The Wizard
AND
The Frog
BOOK 1

RICHARD FIERCE

Dragonfire Press

Cover by germancreative.

ISBN: 978-1-947329-11-9

OTHER BOOKS

The Fallen King Chronicles

Dragonsphere
The Fallen King
The Valiant King
The Restored King

Stand Alone

Oppression
Liberation
Shard of the Sun
Chronicles of Mirstone
The Last Page

CONTENTS

ACKNOWLEDGEMENTS

To all the writers of my favorite comedy movies:

Thank you for the laughs and the inspiration!

CHAPTER ONE

An Unfortunate Meeting

"Damn troll!"

I dove to the ground, narrowly missing the huge axe being swung at me. Dust stung my eyes and I felt the gritty texture of dirt in my mouth. I spit, rolled away from the ugly creature, and scrambled to my feet.

Trolls are generally found far from the borders of a town, usually living in caves or swampy areas. This troll had taken up residence in the sewers of Casem, a small town with a big dream. The Lord of the city had made it his mission to make Casem the jewel of the East. That's not a job I would ever want.

Granted, he probably felt the same about my job. You see, I hunt monsters. Like this troll. And like most trolls, this one was obnoxiously strong. And he knew it.

The beast rushed me, wildly swinging his nicked, rusty battle axe. I brought my sword up and blocked the attack. The force of the troll's strike made my arm go numb and the blade fell uselessly to the ground. I cursed and jumped back to avoid another swing.

Just another problem for me. Let's just say

things in my life weren't going as planned. First, I'd recently lost my girlfriend. I don't mean that she died. I mean that I literally lost her. In the woods. At night. To be fair, it wasn't completely my fault. She'd wandered off from the camp and when I went searching, I didn't see a single sign of her.

So, I left.

It's not like she doesn't know her way around the area. She's lived there most of her life. Besides that, I had already taken the job to come kill this troll. Insofacto, I had to leave. I'm sure she'll be ecstatic to see me when I get back.

I hope.

I dodged to the left and snatched my sword off the ground, then turned to face the beast. The troll was in mid-swing, so I side-stepped the blow and took advantage of the situation by hacking a deep gash along the creature's thigh. It staggered and screeched, but otherwise seemed unfazed by the wound.

Trolls are tough creatures to hurt, and even tougher creatures to kill. Normally, I'd have at least two other hunters with me to take on one of these beasts. And that's the second thing that went wrong. My go-to guys and I had a falling out over … well, that's not important right now. Suffice it to say, I was on my own for this job.

The creature regained its balance and turned to face me. It regarded me with a look of utter contempt. Trolls are ugly beasts. Full-grown, they can be as tall as eight feet and a few hundred pounds of raw muscle. Their skin tone can range from light gray to a sickly green. This troll's skin was a yellowish hue, but not as gross as some trolls I've seen. He also wasn't very tall, standing only a head taller than me.

The chances were high that this was a youngster who had left his tribe and decided to get close to humans for a steady food source. Unfortunately for him, the Lord of Casem quickly realized something was wrong when people started rapidly disappearing. A growing troll can eat a lot. And since they aren't very intelligent creatures, this one had signed his own death warrant by not keeping a low profile.

You live and you learn. Well, sometimes. Sometimes you just die.

It's extremely difficult to kill a troll, even with a team of men. It's hard trying to hack off limbs because that requires you to get close to them. And if you aren't fast enough, *they'll* hack *your* limbs off and eat them while you watch. Once you hack a limb off, you have to immediately burn it with fire. And you have to do it quickly, or the limb will start to reattach itself. Trolls not only hate fire, they fear it. So much so they don't bother to cook their meals.

Which leads to my third problem. I didn't have any fire. I'd brought a torch with me, but the troll had surprised me, and I had dropped the torch in a puddle of water. Or muck. It's entirely possible it could have been piss, considering we were at the entrance of the city sewers. I didn't want to think about that, though. Mainly because after I dropped the torch into it, the troll knocked me into it. The tunic under my chainmail was sticking to my skin and felt slimy.

Annoying, to say the least. Gross if my last guess was correct. I shivered in disgust.

The troll roared angrily and rushed me again. I attempted to side-step it again, but my foot got caught in some thick roots and I fell to the ground on my stomach, the air knocked out of me. I blinked rapidly, trying to clear the tears from my eyes while I tried to convince my body it needed to breathe.

Just as I sucked in a deep lungful of glorious air, it was pushed back out of me as the troll stepped on my back. I cried out involuntarily. I felt the creature's rough, grimy hands grab my arm. It removed its foot and lifted me into the air, turning me around so that it could look me in the eyes. It shook my violently until my sword fell from my grasp. Yet again. Someone should invent something that keeps a man's sword from slipping out of his hands. That would be great.

It chuckled to itself and smiled. Grotesque teeth, worn and yellowed, filled its mouth. And its breath was absolutely rank. It smelled like rotten eggs dipped in … you get the point. I gagged and turned my head, expecting to vomit. Thankfully, I didn't. I hated puking, almost as much as I hated trolls.

The troll tightened its grip on my arm and I felt my bones threatening to break. If only I had the strength of a troll. I'd be quite a hero. I kicked it in the stomach twice, which accomplished nothing. It laughed harder, then tossed me to the ground like a sack of potatoes. I grunted and managed to fall on my back. My handsome face was still safe. If I didn't hurry up and find a way to kill this troll, how I looked would be the least of my worries.

I struggled to my feet, the thought that I might have pushed my luck too far this time buzzing around my brain like an annoying bug. Judging by the soreness in my back already, it was safe to assume I would be bruised like hell tomorrow. I shook my head. This troll was pissing me off. It was time to get serious.

"Hey, ugly!" I shouted. "Did your mother not love you? Is that why you're out here all by yourself?"

I don't know why I bothered. Trolls didn't speak Common, so I was just wasting my breath. Still, it made me feel a little better. I saw my sword lay near the troll's foot. It was too risky to try and grab it. The pain shooting up my back would keep me from moving quick enough. The blasted creature looked like he might just win this one. I was too young to die. My best days were still ahead of me. My future kids were counting on me to spread my seed throughout the land …

Seeds. Roots. Aha! I had it! If I could trip over the roots littering the area, then so could this ugly bastard. I took a few steps toward the troll, a grin plastered over my cocky face. It grunted in amusement and sprinted towards me. I back peddled, lifting my knees high so I didn't inadvertently fall myself.

A few more steps.

Finally, something went right for me. The troll's big feet stomped right through a wad of roots. Most of them snapped under the strength and weight of the troll, but a few held. The expression on the beast's face turned to confusion as it fell forward, smashing hard into the ground before it realized what had happened.

"Yes!" I shouted.

I ran to retrieve my sword, then rushed back to the troll. It was yanking its foot, trying to free itself. And it wasn't paying me any attention at all. I shook my head, almost feeling sorry for the brute. Then I lifted my sword and parted the troll's head from its body. A spray of blood misted into the air. Obviously, something like that would kill anything else. Not a troll, though. Nope, even headless those bastards will get back up and put their head back on.

I've seen it happen before and let me tell you, there's nothing more cringe-worthy than watching a troll's severed head reattach itself to its neck. I shivered again just thinking about it. Reaching down, I grabbed the troll's thin tuft of hair and tossed the head a few feet away. Then I began to hack the limbs free, also tossing them aside. I must admit, this was pretty gruesome, but it was a lot less gruesome than letting the creature continue killing innocent people.

During the last troll death I had taken part in, we'd found half-eaten legs of children. It was something I would never forget. And it was one of the many reasons I continued to hunt monsters down, putting an end to them before they caused anymore trouble. Getting paid was great, too, but I have to sound humble, right?

Once the beast was cut into several large pieces, I pulled some flint from a pouch at my waist and started striking it against my blade. Sparks danced into life, falling onto the troll's filthy skin. It took longer than I wanted to spend doing it, but finally the dried fibers of the troll's pants caught fire and began to burn.

I waited until the entire torso was burning, then I grabbed the head and held it over the flaming body. Its mouth opened and screamed one loud, final cry. It was a disturbing sight to watch as the troll's eyes rolled around, looking this way and that before finally rolling back into its head. I set the head aside and let it burn separately. I didn't want to risk having a flaming troll reattaching itself. I had enough problems.

The arms and legs were next. Once every bit of the creature had caught fire, I felt confident enough to let my guard down a little. I kept my blade unsheathed and walked over to the puddle of muck I dropped my torch in. I fished it out, then swung it around to try and dry it off a bit. Air drying, I liked to call it. Then I stuck it into the flames and waited for it to catch fire. The wet wood crackled and popped in protest but lit up.

The entrance of the sewer was outlined in natural stones, but the inside was crafted from sculpted bricks. I doubted there would be any survivors, for trolls rarely kept prisoners, but I had to check. I held the torch up high with one hand, my sword in the other, and stepped into the darkness. The first thing I noticed was the smell. It was worse than the troll's breath. The next thing I noticed was the scattered bones that littered the ground. Some of them crunched under my boots as I walked.

The tunnel twisted to the right, going further under the city. I decided I wasn't going too far into the sewer. There was no telling what I might find. Besides, I didn't want some fool dumping anything while I happened to be standing under them. I flashed my torch from side to side and saw a small army of rats flee deeper into the shadows.

Rats don't bother me, but you know what does? Flying cockroaches. Those things will make me scream like a woman and run. Thank the gods those things are only found on the island of Drea. I went there on a hunt once and that was all it took for me to decide never to go back. My skin started to crawl remembering those pesky bugs.

Something in the shadows moved. Something much larger than a rat. I held my sword up, ready to strike. A muffled sound echoed throughout the tunnel. I took a few hesitant steps, prepared to find another troll.

"Mmm! Mhmm!"

It sounded like a human. I brought my torch lower and saw it, whatever it was. It appeared to be humanoid, but it was covered in a thick fur. Some sort of creature I'd never seen before. Almond shaped eyed, light skin, almost pale in the torchlight. A cord was wrapped around its face, keeping its mouth constricted. Without thinking, I set my sword down, grabbed the cord, and pulled it out of the creature's mouth.

"Oh, thank the Maker!"

As soon as the thing spoke, I realized it wasn't a thing. It was a male. And judging from its accent, it was an elf.

"You can thank me," I replied with a smirk. "Considering I killed the troll."

"Thank you! Thank the Maker! I'll give thanks to anyone who will take it!"

"What happened to you? How did you get down here?"

"That beast attacked me during the night while I was leaving the Academy and …"

"Academy? Wait, are you—" I paused and held the torch out further. The fur the elf was covered in was actually— "You're hairy, wizard!"

"Yes, I know. This stuff is disgusting! Please, cut me loose!"

I grabbed the handle of my sword and sliced through the matted hair and another cord of rope. The elf still struggled to get free, so I offered my hand and pulled him out of the heap of grossness.

"You saved my life," the elf said, brushing clumps of hair off his clothes. "For that, I owe you.

I will devote my life to you from this day forth until—"

"Wow," I interrupted. "No offense, but I've got a girlfriend back home."

"That's not what I meant," the elf huffed, clearly offended. "I'm indebted to you. So, I will go wherever you go until my debt has been paid."

A wizard indebted to me? I considered the possibilities, the jobs I could take with a magic flinger at my disposal … things were starting to look up!

"I accept your life-debt," I said. "You won't be needed at the Academy, will you?"

"No," the elf answered quickly. "My time there has come to an end."

"Excellent," I grinned. "What's your name?"

"Dormuris."

That was a mouthful. "I'll call you D for short."

"I'd rather you didn't," Dormuris said.

"It's easier for me. Besides, if you are indebted to me, you should be doing anything you can to help me, right?"

"Well, technically—"

"D it is," I said. "Now let's get out of here. This place stinks."

We left the sewer and stepped back into fresh air. I took a deep breath and tried to clear the stench from my nose. I noticed one of the troll's arms slowly crawling towards its body, its thick fingers "walking," reminding me of a spider. I skewered the arm with my blade and deposited it next to one of the legs that was still aflame.

"You hacked it to pieces," Dormuris said, eyes wide.

"That I did."

"How did you manage that?"

"It was easy enough," I lied. "I've done this song and dance a few times before. I hunt monsters for a living."

Dormuris looked at me. "You're a hunter?" he asked slowly.

"That's right."

"Oh gods."

"Don't worry," I said. "I don't hunt dragons or giants. Just the smaller, less dangerous sorts."

Dormuris breathed a sigh of relief. "That's good to hear. I was afraid … well, it doesn't matter. Since the troll is dead, where are you headed now?"

"Home," I answered. "My girlfriend is waiting impatiently for me to get back."

I hope.

《—》

"You!"

I stepped inside the house to find my girlfriend,

Pemeria, staring at me in surprise. She was in the middle of cooking something that smelled absolutely delicious.

"Pemeria, my love!" I greeted.

"You've got some nerve," she sputtered. "How dare you come back here after you left me in the woods!"

Uh oh. She could get as crazy as a badger, so I lifted my hands placatingly. "I'm sorry," I said. "You knew I took the job to kill the troll, so I had to leave. It's not like you didn't know how to get home."

"Oh, so it's my fault?"

I wasn't sure how to answer that, so I said, "Yes?"

The clay plate she hurled at me barely missed my head. I heard the air thrum as it whizzed by and crashed into the wall behind me.

"I mean, no," I corrected. That answer seemed to be worse, for the next thing she threw at me was much larger.

"I almost died, woman! What do you want from me?"

"Oh, you almost died? So did I!"

"What happened?" I asked. Now I felt like a fool.

"I tripped and broke my shoe! If a bear or something would have seen me at such a weak state, who knows what could've happened?"

I groaned inwardly. Every time I thought Pemeria couldn't get any crazier, she proved me wrong. "Well, I think my near-death experience was much closer than yours, considering a troll tried to crush me."

"So, this is how you treat me?" she demanded.

"Oh gods, woman," I moaned.

Another plate; followed by another. Now I was having to dodge them. A large expensive vase was next. It shattered, sending fragments everywhere. When she got into these moods, she could break almost everything in the house. I needed some outside help on this one.

"D! Get in here! I need some help!"

The elf came scrambling inside, looking about wildly. "What is it?"

"Angry girlfriend," I replied, dodging a spoon. "A little help?"

Dormuris nodded and began chanting in a strange language. A green light began to glow between his hands. It pulsed and expanded, then hovered lazily across the room until it reached Pemeria. The light contracted, then burst into tiny specks and faded.

"What was that—"

The entire house rumbled for a moment, then everything went still. Pemeria was gone. I looked to Dormuris, then back to where Pemeria had been.

"Uh … Pemeria?"

"Oh no," Dormuris muttered.

"What's that?" I asked, starting to get worried.

"Well, what happened was … I intended to cast a shield around you, but instead …"

"Instead what?" I asked. A few steps brought me around the cabinets to find a large green frog sitting on the floor. I raised my brow and looked at Dormuris.

He smiled nervously.

"Where's Pemeria?" I asked.

"You're looking at her."

"The frog?" I asked incredulously.

The elf nodded. "Yeah, about that …"

"Why would you turn her into a frog?" I demanded.

"It was an accident. Magic is tougher than it looks. And not everyone has a knack for it, so …"

"I thought you said you are a wizard."

"I am," Dormuris said. "Sort of."

CHAPTER TWO

A Golden Quest

"Sort of? What does that mean?"

"Well, I can sometimes control the magic to do what I want. A lot of times, though, things like this happen."

"Seriously?"

"Yes."

We stared at each other in silence. I was trying to wrap my mind around a wizard who wasn't that good with magic. It was difficult. Actually, it was impossible. I couldn't wrap my mind around it.

"How did you finish your time at the Academy?" I asked.

"They kicked me out," Dormuris answered. "They called me a 'liability.' That's rubbish. I just need more time to perfect my skills, that's all."

"Well, I think you've done enough damage here. Seeing as how Pemeria is a frog now, I'm sure she's going to be even more angry than she was as a human. You can leave now."

"I can't," Dormuris said.

"You can't what?"

"I can't leave. I've sworn a life-debt to you, and you accepted it."

"So? Take it back."

"It doesn't work like that."

"What do you mean?" I asked.

"A life-debt is a form of magic," Dormuris explained. "The word of an elf is magical, which is why we don't lightly use them."

"So how do we break the spell?"

"Once I've paid my debt, the spell will go away."

Well, well, well. It seems that things *weren't* actually going my way. Instead, they had just gotten far worse. Not only was Pemeria a frog now, but I also was stuck with an elven wizard who sucked at magic and was bound to me until he saved my life. Great. Just great. I sighed.

"Fine. Change her back."

Dormuris smiled thinly.

"Are you kidding me right now?"

"Sorry," his face scrunched in mock agony. "I didn't mean to turn her into one, so I have no idea how to turn her back into a human."

"Wow. You're a really helpful wizard, you know that?"

Dormuris shrugged. "You said do something. I tried."

I laughed in frustration and shook my head, then knelt in front of the frog that was Pemeria.

"I'll find a way to get you changed back," I said softly. I hoped she could understand me.

"You damn well better," Pemeria's voice came out of the frog's mouth.

I fell backwards in surprise. "Did you just talk?"

"You're lucky I'm a frog at the moment," Pemeria threatened. "I'd love to smack you over the head right now."

Even better. My gods, could the day get any worse?

There was a knock at the door.

"Can you get that?" I asked D.

The elf opened the door and an older man stepped inside. He was dirty, but not like a homeless person. The dirt that covered him was from the road, and from the amount of dirt on him, he must have traveled a long way.

"Jack?" The man asked.

"That's me," I replied.

"Thank goodness! We need your help!"

"I'm in the middle of something," I said.

"But we're being terrorized by a monster!"

"There's a few people I know who can help you out. If you've got problems with a goblin or an orc, these people can take care of you. And they charge less than I do, too."

"Oh no, sir. We do not have problems with an orc or a goblin. The wicked creature that haunts us is much more powerful."

"A troll?"

"No, sir. A vampire!"

I was fairly certain my heart fell into my stomach. *A vampire?* Gods above! I'd never seen one, but I knew they existed. Creatures of darkness, able to use magic without words. They lived in darkness, creating misery and fear wherever they went.

"I ..." I frowned. It was my oath to fight monsters, but Pemeria was a frog right now. Priorities. Decisions. This was too stressful.

"Please, sir. She commands the darkness. She's ensorcelled seven dwarven miners to do her bidding and controls the animals. Our children, sir ... some of them have gone missing."

The image of the half-eaten limbs of children from my old troll job came back to me, haunting me. I couldn't let these people down. I looked at Pemeria, her green flesh slick and slimy. I'd have to figure out what to do with her.

"I'll come," I answered the old man. "Where is your town?"

"A week's ride north," he answered. "The city of Thurm. We're ruled by Lord Skrinn."

"I know it," I answered. "I have to arrange some

things, but I will be there as soon as possible.”

“Thank you, sir! Thank you!”

Dormuris walked the man out and shut the door behind them.

“You know I have to do this,” I said to Pemeria.

“I know,” she replied. “But you need to get me changed back first.”

“I don’t know if I can,” I said.

“You don’t have a choice.”

That tone in her voice made me aware that she was not happy. When Dormuris came back inside, I looked at him.

“We’re going to the Academy,” I announced.

“Why exactly?”

“Why do you think?” I asked. “There’s real wizards there. We’ll get one of them to turn Pemeria back and then we’ll go help the people of Thurm.”

“I don’t think the Academy is going to help,” Dormuris said.

“They have to. They can’t just leave her as a frog.”

“I suppose it’s worth a try,” Dormuris said. “Though I have heard of something that turned someone back into a human once.”

“What?”

“There’s a story of someone who once kissed a

frog and the frog turned into a man. Pemeria is a woman, obviously, but it might still work."

"That's a true story?" I asked.

"Absolutely," Dormuris said.

"Right." I looked at Pemeria, who looked up at me. If she knew that I was thinking about how I *didn't* want to kiss her right now, she'd probably kill me. I picked her up, cupping her gently in my hands and held my breath. I tried to picture Pemeria in her human form and pretend that I was kissing her normal self.

I closed my eyes and leaned my head down. Another inch and her slimy skin would touch my lips. I pecked her on the head, then turned and spat. When I looked back at her, Pemeria was glaring at me. Well, as much of a glare as a frog could muster.

"It didn't work," I grunted, not surprised. I was going to kill this elf.

"At least your tried, right?"

I glared at Dormuris. "Let's get to the Academy. The longer Pemeria stays a frog, the longer she's going to hate me."

I gently placed Pemeria into a pouch at my waist and left the house. Dormuris followed, whether because the spell forced him to or because he wanted to, I didn't know. Thankfully, Casem was only a half-hour trek from our rural town. I was exhausted. My muscles ached from exertion and from the blows the troll had struck, and now my brain hurt from thinking.

"If your magic always does this, what exactly did you do that got you kicked out of the Academy?" I asked, curious.

"That's a long story," Dormuris answered.

"We've got a decent walk. Start talking."

"I accidentally summoned a dragon," he said sheepishly.

"That's it?"

"Well, no. The dragon set fire to part of the town and it took several of the head masters to banish it."

"What were you actually trying to do?" I asked, almost afraid to hear the answer.

"Change water into wine."

"That's a massive difference in results," I said, shaking my head in disbelief.

Dormuris didn't say anything in reply. I almost felt bad for the guy. He clearly had the calling for magic, but for whatever reason, it just didn't work for him. That, or he didn't know how to control it. With all the training the Academy offered, it would seem that control shouldn't be the issue. Well, regardless of what the underlying issue was, the faster he could repay his debt and be on his way, the better.

We spent the rest of the walk in silence. I occasionally heard Pemeria cursing from my pouch, but I tried to ignore that. If we couldn't find a wizard who could restore her back to normal, my life was going to be a mess. Besides not getting married and having kids, what was I supposed to do with her? Set her loose in a pond somewhere? Gods, it was too much to worry about.

Casem's borders came into view and the city guards let us in with bored expressions on their faces. I led the way towards the Academy, a large square-shaped building on the northern end of the city. Casem wasn't huge, but it was rapidly growing. People of all races were moving here, hoping to be part of the city lord's dream in making the city the jewel of the East. I still didn't know exactly what he meant by that.

The Academy was surrounded by a mix of stone walls and iron gates. Two guards stood at the entrance, but these weren't city guards. These men wore the robes of wizards and wielded staffs. Not very imposing unless you knew what a wizard was capable of. And I was well aware of what they could do. Dormuris aside, I'd spent plenty of time in the presence of a few wizards. Most of them were self-absorbed, greedy, power hungry, and absolutely insane. Mostly insane.

While Dorumuris seemed to defy that trend, his downfall was his inability to control his magic. If it weren't for that, he might be the perfect partner to hunt monsters with.

"Do you have an appointment?" one of the guards asked as we approached.

"No," I answered. "I need to see someone about reversing a spell."

"What kind of spell?" the second guard asked.

The two looked as dissimilar as a bird and a snake. The first guard who spoke had a shaved head, brown eyes, and a thin goatee beginning to sprout from his chin. He was skinny, and his robes looked too big for him. The other one was an older man, with graying hair and blue eyes that seemed to hold his years within them. They seemed like reasonable men, so I was hoping they would let us in without issue.

"Well," I pulled Pemeria out of my pouch. "This is my girlfriend."

The guards exchanged glances, and the older man smiled. "We don't do *that* kind of magic here."

"No, of course not," I laughed. "I meant, this is what my girlfriend was turned into. She was a human, but this one," I nodded toward Dormuris, "turned her into a frog."

The younger guard seemed to recognize Dormuris and his eyes widened. "Gods," he breathed. "You must have horrible luck to have come in contact with him."

"Lately, it seems like I don't have any luck," I answered. "Do you think someone can help me out?"

The young guard shook his head. "I wouldn't know where to begin."

The older man examined Pemeria intently. "Can she speak?" he asked.

"Yes, I can speak just fine," Pemeria answered smugly.

"Interesting," the old man said. "It's rare that a shapeshifting spell can allow a person to keep their ability to speak. Give me a minute and I'll see if I can get you an audience with one of our masters."

"Thank you," I said. "I really appreciate that."

The guard went inside the gates and soon disappeared inside the building. The younger guard stayed put, keeping a wary eye on Dormuris.

"You heard what he did, didn't you?" he whispered to me.

"Something about a dragon?" I asked.

The man nodded. "That's not all, though. That was the last straw for the head master. He's caused all sorts of mischief."

"Like what?"

"Well, he once turned a statue of the head master into a golem."

"What's a golem?" I asked.

"It's like an elemental but it doesn't occur naturally. It's basically a living creature made of stone or clay. It nearly destroyed half the east wing and almost killed a student."

I didn't know what an elemental was, either, but I got the point. The more I heard about Dormuris's misguided magic, the more I started to worry he was going to put me into a bad situation. Well, I was already in a bad situation. A *worse* situation, then. If I were battling a monster and he cast a spell accidentally, who knows what could happen. I was starting to think I should be afraid for my life with him around.

A few minutes later, the older guard returned. He eyed Dormuris curiously, then looked at me. "Well, most of the masters declined to help, mainly because of your friend here."

"That's just wonderful," I groaned.

"There is one who agreed to see you, but I have to warn you."

He looked at his younger counterpart and they shared some sort of knowing look. "Master Zalore is a bit of an oddity. He has some quirks that are best left overlooked."

"I can do that. I deal with all sorts of oddities in my line of work," I said. The guards were quiet, so I assumed they were waiting on an explanation. "I hunt monsters," I added.

"Ah," they said in unison.

"Right then, follow me and I'll escort you to his office."

The younger guard continued to stare at Dormuris mistrustfully, but they allowed him to come too. We walked behind the older wizard in single file and I stared at everything. I'd never been inside the Academy before, so every sight was new to me. We traveled along narrow corridors, up huge flights of steps, and finally through a vast hall that contained a door every twenty feet. I assumed these were the offices of the masters. Most of them were shut. The one we stopped at was open.

The old man knocked anyway, and a voice within told us to come in. The guard waved us in, but he stayed outside. Once inside, he shut the door and we stood in the most bizarrely decorated room I'd ever seen. Multi-colored rugs covered the floors, their bright, vivid colors a stark contrast to the dark and plain tapestries hanging on the walls. There was a table covered in globes of clear glass, beakers and burners, and all sorts of gadgets that appeared to have gears and cogwheels that allowed them to operate.

Master Zalore appeared to have a love for the extraordinary. That wasn't so peculiar. Perhaps his trinkets, foreign and different, made his fellows think he too was the odd one out. I shrugged and turned my attention to him—Master Zalore—who sat behind a huge desk made of oak wood. It was covered with books and pieces of parchment, all of which were scattered about haphazardly.

"Welcome," he greeted. He stood up and I realized why I hadn't noticed him when we first entered the room. His clothing was the exact same color, and design, as his chair. It was like he was wearing a camouflage of sorts.

"Hello," I replied. I tilted my head in greeting, not sure how exactly to show respect to a wizard.

"I hear you have a problem most distressing."

"Yes, I do. Dormuris here turned my girlfriend into a frog."

Master Zalore nodded. "I heard. And you have come here looking to have it reversed. I completely understand. Magic is a fickle mistress, one that can quickly change its loyalty from doing what *you* need to doing what *it* wants. I can help to change the frog back into her human state, but I am going to need a few things. Things that you will need to retrieve."

I focused on every word he said. This man was going to be my savior, so I wanted to make sure I heard every detail.

"Absolutely," I said. "Anything you need."

"Good, good," he replied. "The things I need will not be easy to possess, so take heed that you use caution."

"I'm used to dealing with danger. I hunt monsters for a living, so …" I felt like I didn't need to finish that sentence.

Master Zalore grinned at me. His top incisors shined with gold and silver. The left one was silver and the right one was gold, but on the bottom portion of his mouth, the metals were reversed. It looked strange to me, but who cared? So long as he could get Pemeria back to normal, that was all I cared about.

"Even so," the master wizard continued, "I must warn you about the hazards involved. I don't want your blood on my hands if something befalls you, any of you."

"Understandable," I said. "I accept any and all

risks."

"Good. I need a golden egg and a unicorn."

I stared at the man and waited for him to laugh, crack a smile or imply in some way that he was joking. When he didn't, I cleared my throat and scratched my chin. Small, dry flakes of skin covered my finger tips and I brushed them off on my pants.

"Uh … a golden egg?" I asked.

"And a unicorn," Master Zalore said. "Don't forget the unicorn. That's the most important part."

"Right." I paused, my brain still tired and stressed from Dormuris's rogue spell on my girlfriend. "Where exactly do I get a golden egg or a unicorn?"

"Far to the south is a mountain that rises above everything around it. Within that mountain is a vast maze of tunnels filled with traps of every conceivable type. Beyond those traps is a magical creature, a goose, that lays golden eggs. It's guarded by minotaurs, who have kept the goose under tight watch for years. They melt down the eggs and cast their own coins and have built a tremendous wealth for themselves. That is where you must go to find the golden egg."

"Wait, are you talking about the Minotaur Triad?"

"The same."

I groaned. This was going to be harder than I thought. The Minotaur Triad was an organized crime syndicate, one whose power and cruelty were to be respected, if not feared. Everyone knew they had more wealth than King Edwin himself, but there weren't many who knew where they got it from. It seems Master Zalore has done his homework.

"It's a suicide mission," I said. "*If* we were able to even get inside their fortress, there's no telling how long it would take to navigate their tunnels. It's been purposefully designed to lead people into traps, all to protect their goose."

"Hence my disclaimer about danger," Master Zalore replied. "If you can't retrieve the items I need, then your girlfriend will have to remain a frog. And that wouldn't be good for anyone, least of all her. Shape-shifting can be addictive to the wizards who practice it. If they spend too much time in a different state, eventually they won't be able to change back."

"What are you saying?" I asked, feeling dread worm its way into my stomach.

"If your girlfriend remains a frog too long, I won't be able to change her back. No one will."

Gods above, I cursed.

"Well, that's great. In the unbelievable chance that we manage to rip off the Minotaur Triad, where the hell do we find a unicorn? I thought they were all dead."

Master Zalore ran his hand through his long white beard, easily a foot in length. "I think you should focus your attention on the egg for now. The unicorn is less of an issue in regard to reaching it. If you are willing to retrieve the egg, I can speed up your journey by transporting you to the outskirts of their mountain. Too close, and they will assume the Academy took part in this. That's a liability I cannot risk."

I started to consider that Master Zalore was not "officially" allowed to do anything like this. That was his problem, though, not mine.

"I will go. Can Pemeria stay here under your care?" I asked.

"I'm afraid not," he answered. "I have too many duties to attend to and I would hate for her to get lost or stepped on."

Great. I guess I was going to have to take her with me.

"I assume you will need some supplies. Dormuris can take you to the armory. There's also a pantry there, so collect what you need, and I will get the portal ready."

We left Master Zalore's chamber and Dormuris took the lead. We went back the way we'd come, down the massive staircase and then down another stairwell that led further below the ground level of the Academy. A colossal set of wooden doors is where we ended up. Two men, barely into their teens, struggled to open the doors. They eventually managed to budge one enough that we could fit through.

The armory was surprisingly small. The chamber had less room than Master Zalore's office, but the weapons offered were incredible. I found a sword in flawless condition and picked it up to examine it. The hilt was wrapped in black leather and the pommel was a rounded blue stone. Left to guess, I assumed it was a sapphire. The guard and the blade itself appeared to be made of silver, but I knew it couldn't be real silver. The blade had a gleaming sheen to it. It was beautiful, but I knew it wouldn't look that nice after I used it.

"Take it," Dormuris said, eyeing me. "It's a magnificent weapon."

"I don't want to ruin it," I said.

"Don't worry about that," the elf replied. "It's imbued with powerful spells. It will serve you much better than the weapon you have now."

I debated only a moment more before pulling my blade free and sheathing the new one.

"What do I do with mine?" I asked.

"Leave it here. Someone may fix it up."

I shrugged and left the blade in the spot I'd found the new one in, then headed into the pantry. It was fairly common stuff. Dried jerky, water skins, things that were perfect for long journeys. I grabbed several pieces of the jerky and stuffed them into a sack, then added two waterskins. The sack had a strap, and I slung it over my shoulder.

"You ready?" I asked Dormuris.

"As ready as I can be," he answered.

We made our way back to Master Zalore's chamber and found him waiting for us, an impatient air about him.

"That took long enough," he muttered. "The portal has been open too long already. Hurry through before the minotaurs catch the scent of my magic."

We hurried over to the portal, which was a swirling watery mist on the floor. Flashes of light flickered amidst the whirling mass, making it look like a storm. I adjusted the strap of the sack and looked at Master Zalore.

"Once you get outside of the Triad's realm, use this to get back here." The old wizard handed me a circular pendant made of wood. It was roughly the size of two coins put together. "Think of where you want to be and break it. The spell will activate and take you to the place you are thinking about, as long as it's a real place."

"Anything else I need to know?"

He came to stand behind us and placed a hand on my shoulder.

"Yes," he answered. "Don't die."

And then he shoved me into the watery maelstrom.

CHAPTER THREE

Hooves and Horns

The magical portal pulled and pushed at me, battering me with powerful force.

I had the dreadful feeling of falling, the sensation where you feel your stomach leap. I opened my mouth to scream, but if any sound came out, it was lost in the twirling, shifting mass of magic. There was a rushing sound, like that of an approaching wind, and then the portal was gone. A jarring stop to the falling sensation, and then I realized I was lying on my back staring up into the blue sky above.

My eyes were slightly disoriented, and my stomach had settled down, but I felt shaky. I risked trying to sit up and everything seemed to correct itself. I looked over to my right and saw Dormuris standing, his eyes turned toward the mountain that loomed in the distance. It drew my attention, too. I'd seen the home of the minotaurs only once before when I rode with my hunter friends Theo and Breg, the two I was no longer on good terms with.

Still, despite seeing the mountain before, it was awe inspiring. The rest of the landscape was flowing fields of green grass and flowers. Standing in the midst of all the greenery was the mountain, an enormous red beast.

"So, that's where we're headed?" Dormuris asked, turning to face me.

"Yes." I tried to get up and the elf rushed over to offer me his hand. I took it and pulled myself up onto my feet. "Thanks," I said. I checked my pouch and found that Pemeria was still there. Still angry too, but undamaged. The pendant Master Zalore gave me was on the ground by my feet. I knelt and picked it up, then slipped it into my boot.

"Now, we have to figure out a way to get inside. If they see us, they are likely to kill us on sight without any warnings or questions at all. Have you ever seen a minotaur before?" I asked the elf.

"Only in books. Drawings and such."

"Well, forget what you might think you know. They are cruel, viciously strong, and don't care about anything other than their gold. They have built an empire of crime. If we are caught, we can forget about anything we might have wanted to do in life. If they don't kill us, they'll force us into slavery. How does that sound?"

"Intimidating," Dormuris replied. "And not at all how I want my life to end."

"Good. So, what are our options?"

"Magic."

"Say what now?" I asked. "I've seen how your spells work out, and I can say right now that suggestion should go right into the garbage."

"Hear me out," Dormuris said, ignoring my insult. "I can use an illusion to make us look like minotaurs. That'll make it much easier to get inside. Trust me."

"That's a terrible idea," I said. Both his idea *and* Dormuris expecting me to trust him.

"If the spell works, we'll look like minotaurs. We'll be able to walk right in instead of sneaking around," Dormuris replied.

"That *if* is a big problem. What happens when your spell doesn't work and something worse than this happens?" I waved my hand at my pouch, at Pemeria. "Then we're screwed."

"What's *your* plan to get inside their base of operations?"

I assumed Dormuris might ask this question, but I hadn't the slightest clue as to how we could get in without being seen. As much as I didn't like it, I was afraid we would have to rely on Dormuris's chaotic magic to get us in. I gave in.

"Fine, we'll put our lives in your hands."

"Oh gods," Pemeria's muffled voice groaned.

"It'll work," Dormuris said. The conviction in his voice was almost enough to sway me to believe him. Every time I thought of Permeria, I cringed at what might happen. Minotaurs are tough, violent creatures. Even with a band of men, it would be difficult to handle a single one. The fact we were going into an area that had dozens was a death wish.

We began the trek towards the mountain. I kept myself focused, checking for lookouts or anything out of the ordinary. So far, so good. Perhaps *too* good. I decided not to let my mind wander and worry about things I had no control over. We reached the base of the mountain and I stared up at the imposing wonder. Every rock and crevice was a reddish hue, like the skin of a demon had been tossed over the thing. High above, the dark silhouette of a cave entrance was barely visible.

I looked at Dormuris. This was going to be difficult, much more so with the elf potentially causing a disaster.

"Don't do anything unless I tell you to," I said. "No spells, no rough movements. A single loose rock could cause an avalanche, and that's the last thing we need."

"Got it," Dormuris replied, nodding firmly.

It took an hour of climbing to reach the cave that served as the entrance to the minotaur hideout. A three-foot ledge extended from the opening, serving as a natural landing of sorts. I pulled myself over the lip of rock and then reached out to help Dormuris up. I brushed the dust off my clothes, then looked in my pouch to make sure Pemeria didn't get squished. She was still there, and still angry. I smiled at her, and as she opened her mouth to say something, closed the pouch.

"Right, let's get to it then. Start casting, wizard."

Dormuris nodded and closed his eyes, then

raised his arms up and began whispering in his strange magical language. I could feel a slight tingle against my skin, like the feeling you have when there's a stray hair touching you. It was faint, and the feeling passed quickly.

The elf opened his eyes and smiled. "It worked!" he said excitedly.

"Judging by your enthusiasm, it seems you even doubt yourself," I said dryly. "How do *I* know it worked?"

"Look at your reflection," Dormuris answered.

I drew my blade and held it up before my face. The gruesome visage of a minotaur stared back at me.

"Wow," I said, watching my beastly mouth move but hearing my voice. "That's a ridiculous amount of detail."

Dormuris shrugged, but I could see him beaming with pride. He closed his eyes and repeated the spell, and I watched in surprise as the false appearance slowly took shape over him. His minotaur illusion was taller than mine, and his horns were larger, too. I sheathed my blade.

"How do I look?" he asked.

"It'll work," I answered. "What about our voices? If we speak, it'll be obvious we aren't who we appear to be."

"I can't do anything about that," the elf said. "We'll have to either disguise our voices or not speak at all."

"That's great. Mute minotaurs. Should I hurl myself off the ledge now, or after I push you off?"

"Neither," Dormuris said. "We can do this. I know it's my fault you are in this mess, but I am here to help get things right."

"Yeah, because that life-debt spell forces you to be."

"Even if it didn't," Dormuris said. "I'd still be here helping you."

I didn't say anything. It *was* his fault, but I was starting to feel bad for insulting him. He was trying to fix his mistake, so I had to give him credit for that.

"I appreciate that," I finally forced myself to say. "Once we're inside, we'll have to navigate these tunnels carefully. From everything I've heard, the Triad has all sorts of nasty death traps in here. One wrong decision and we're dead."

"Then let's not make any bad decisions," Dormuris smiled. "Let's go, daylight is burning."

A few feet into the cave and we were thrown into pitch black darkness. I held my hands out in front of me in case I bumped into anything before my eyes adjusted. Slowly, things began to come into focus. The outline of the cave's walls, the rocky floor, and ahead, the light of torches along the walls.

It seemed odd to me that we hadn't encountered

any guards yet, but as I considered it, I figured maybe the Triad had enough to their reputation that most would-be thieves didn't want to die and steered clear of the place. They were smarter than us.

The tunnel ran for a few hundred feet, then branched off in two directions. I stopped and looked at every detail I could to determine which way might be correct.

"Left or right?" I asked Dormuris.

"Right," he answered.

I stared at the dusty floor of both channels. The right one seemed to have more dust on the floor, which would lead me to assume it was much less traveled.

"We're going left," I announced.

"To spite me, or …"

"No. Look closely at the floor. The left has less dust, and I think I can even see a partial hoofprint. This way is traveled more."

Dormuris knelt and stared intently for a moment, then rose to his feet.

"You're right," he said. "I would never have thought to look at that."

"You're a wizard, not a hunter. These are things I've learned over the years. Lack of attention has led too many in my profession dying an early death."

"That's not surprising, considering you track

monsters down."

"Step carefully. Although this seems the correct way, that doesn't mean they don't have traps setup."

I stayed in the lead and investigated heavily every few steps. Half an hour in, I knew it was taking too long. We still hadn't seen anyone, but there were sounds of activity beginning to echo into the tunnel. At our current rate of productivity, it was going to take us hours to make any progress.

"This isn't working," I said softly. "Either we'll need to split up or we need to pick up the pace."

"I think splitting up is a bad idea."

"So do I. I'll walk faster, but it's going to increase the risk. Just try to help me catch any traps before they kill us, yeah?"

The tunnel abruptly turned to the right and we almost collided with a lone minotaur. The creature easily stood over six feet tall. Its horns were long and pointed, and it sported a large metal ring in its septum. A harness on its back held a massive battle axe in place. The creature was facing us, but it wasn't paying attention at first. I managed to put a scowl on my face as the beast looked at me.

"What're you doing?" a deep baritone voice spoke. His words echoed throughout the tunnel.

I tried my best to make voice deep and rough. "All clear down there," I answered.

The minotaur looked like it frowned. "Who told you to patrol the entrance?"

I exchanged looks with Dormuris. I was clueless about minotaur names. Thankfully, I didn't have to guess as the creature shook his head.

"It doesn't matter," he boomed. "It was probably that new idiot, Dadak. Do yourself a favor. Don't listen to that one. He won't be here much longer if he keeps on screwing things up."

"Got it," I answered. "I heard he's a real pain in the hoof."

The minotaur grunted. "Yeah, whatever." He turned around. I smiled at Dormuris and we passed him and continued down the tunnel. The sound of voices, laughter, and the occasional scream were becoming common place.

"How long will this illusion last?" I asked.

"I don't know," Dormuris replied.

I was beyond hoping that we'd make it out of here alive at this point, so I just nodded and kept walking. There were long stretches of tunnel where we didn't see or hear anyone. At one particular side channel, we almost fell into a pit filled with sharpened steel spikes. I'd missed the fake flooring and nearly tumbled in with it as it collapsed beneath me. I'd reached for the wall and scraped my knuckles before catching myself. The dull throb was more annoying than painful.

My heart was hammering in my chest now and I got hot and sweaty. There was just something about dying that really made me nervous. It felt like we had been walking for hours, and we probably had been, but it was impossible to judge the passage of time in here.

"It would be great if we had some sort of directions to guide us," I complained.

"Oh! Master Zalore gave me this." Dormuris dug into his pack and withdrew a rolled-up parchment. He unfurled it and held it up for me to see. I had to squint in the faint light, but it appeared to be a map.

"What is it?" I asked.

"It's a map of the tunnels," Dormuris answered. He seemed proud to have it.

"Are you serious? We've been wandering around in here for who knows how long and you've had a map the *entire* time?"

I was going to kill him. I was definitely going to kill this elf.

"Sorry, I forgot I had it. I've been focused on keeping this illusion spell going."

"I thought you said you didn't know how long it would last?"

"I don't. It depends on how quickly it exhausts me. So far, it's not too taxing."

I sighed. Why couldn't anything in my life go right? Just once. Just once, I would like for *something* to go right. I took the map from the elf and read over it, trying to decipher where we might be and where we should go next. There were small X's drawn at random spots, and I began to suspect those were symbols for traps. I stepped out of the side-channel and then compared the direction of the main tunnel to the map.

"I know where we are," I said. "Come on, this way. Surprisingly, we're almost there."

The map made navigating the tunnels much easier. I still couldn't believe Dormuris could forget he had a map to the place. This guy was a real—

"Stop!" Dormuris's voiced suddenly hissed.

I paused and looked back at him. "What is it?" I whispered back.

He pointed ahead. Along the ceiling of the tunnel, mostly hidden by shadows, were at least a dozen steel tipped spears. They were pointed toward the floor. I checked the map and confirmed there was no X.

"This must be new," I said. "It's not on the map anywhere."

"Are we in the right spot?"

I nodded. "Yes. Everything else matches. Around the corner should be a door. Inside we should find the goose."

Hope was starting to blossom. Granted, we still had to steal an egg and escape, but we were almost halfway done with this insane quest.

"That looks like a trap to me," Dormuris said. "The question is, how does it get set off and how do we get past it?"

I knelt and studied to the floor. There didn't

appear to be any trip wires or loose stones that would trigger the spears to fall. I stood up and examined the walls next. Again, nothing that I could see.

"I'm not sure," I finally said. "I can't find any sort of trigger. Whoever designed this is damnably clever."

"What do we do?"

I held the map up near a torch and tried to find another way. There wasn't one. I folded the map and handed it to the elf.

"Looks like this is the only way," I answered. I tightened the strap on my sack and prepared myself mentally to go under a canopy of death. "We're going to run through it."

"Run?" Dormuris asked. I could tell by his tone he had the same trepidation I did.

"Yes. Don't let anything slow you down. Ready?"

"No, but if this is the only way, then let's do it."

"That's the spirit," I said. "On three. One, two–"

Without waiting for three, Dormuris sprinted forward. I quickly followed after him. My instincts were telling me to look up, but I knew that could seal my fate. If I tripped or slowed down, it could be the last thing I ever did. We made it out from under the spears, and I expected a loud clamor.

Nothing.

I stopped and turned to see the spears were still

suspended in place. That seemed odd, but I wasn't going to question our luck. I turned back and saw Dormuris was standing in front of a large door.

"This is it," I said softly, coming to stand beside him.

"There's no telling what's on the other side of this door," Dormuris said. "It could be a small army, or it could be empty."

"Only one way to find out," I said. We grabbed onto the steel ring that served as the door handle and pulled with all our might. The door groaned in protest as it slowly opened. As soon as it was cracked enough that we could fit inside, we released the handle. The door stayed put.

"Here we go," I whispered. I drew my sword and stepped inside the doorway. That's when I felt it. A trip wire snapped under the weight of my foot. A few seconds later, the spears dropped from the ceiling and crashed to the floor, and the tunnel reverberated with a loud noise.

There wasn't a doubt in my mind that sound was going to alert someone, probably a guard. Several guards. The entire Triad. I grabbed Dormuris with my free hand and pulled him into the room with me.

The room was illuminated with both torches and a myriad of candles. In the back of the chamber, centered against the wall, was a bulky nest. And in that nest was the largest goose I had ever seen. It was easily as tall as me and as wide as two minotaurs standing side by side. It was clearly overweight.

Standing beside the nest was a lone minotaur. He didn't seem to notice us, and the goose looked bored. I let go of Dormuris and held up my blade, prepared to fight off the vicious creature. The minotaur slowly turned his head toward us, but his stance didn't seem threatening.

"Who's there?" he asked.

Could he not see us? I advanced slowly, my blade ready to impale the creature through the heart if I saw the faintest movement. Roughly ten feet away, I realized why the beast didn't seem bothered. Its eyes were covered in a milky-white glaze.

It was blind.

"It's just me," I said, disguising my voice. "I'm here to collect an egg."

"You're early," the blind minotaur replied. "The goose won't be popping anything out for another few minutes."

"I know, but Dadak is impatient."

The minotaur snorted. "Dadak. That bastard's going to take an axe to the back if he doesn't learn his place."

That made two of the creatures we encountered who had a mutual disdain for whoever Dadak was. I made a mental note of that, thinking it might come in handy later.

"Yeah, well, what can you do?" I grunted.

The blind minotaur stood silently for a moment, then asked, "How did you manage to trip the wire? You've been here plenty of times."

My brain scrambled for a response, but I didn't have one.

"It was me," Dormuris answered. "I didn't see it."

"Who're you?" the minotaur asked.

"He's new," I said. "One of Dadak's guys."

"Keep your mouth shut about what I said," the creature threatened. "Dadak's gaining a lot of enemies. It'd be best for you if you didn't hold tightly to your reigns of loyalty to him."

"Noted," Dormuris said.

The giant goose stood up and began to shuffle around.

"She's getting ready," the minotaur announced.

The goose twisted its head this way and that, then blinked lazily. A loud thud, then the bird sat down.

"Go ahead," the minotaur said.

I walked up to the nest and eyed the bird warily. Since I didn't know anything about the Triad's gold enterprise, I assumed the bird was used to having its eggs taken, but I knew what could happen when one assumed. I stepped into the nest and carefully walked behind the goose. My eyes widened in shock.

The egg was the length of my arm and almost as wide as my chest. When I thought egg, I was thinking something much smaller. How the hell were we supposed to get out of here carrying something that huge? I looked at Dormuris and motioned for him to help me.

"I'm going to have the new guy take this one," I said.

The minotaur shrugged.

Dormuris climbed into the nest and I lowered my voice.

"Look at this! It's huge. How are we going to get this thing out of here?"

"How heavy is it?"

"I don't know. Considering it's made of gold, I'm going to guess pretty heavy."

Dormuris grabbed the egg by the sides and heaved. He was able to lift it with a little difficulty. "It's not too bad," he grunted. "It's not light, but it's not as heavy as I expected, either."

"Well, we still have to find a way to get it out of here without being noticed. Carrying a huge egg isn't exactly subtle."

"What's taking you so long?" the blind creature questioned.

"Sorry," I answered. "New guy here is having some trouble."

"Figures," the minotaur muttered. "Dadak attracts the idiots."

"Screw it," I said to Dormuris. "We'll just take it and get out of here as quickly as possible. We don't have time to stand here trying to figure things out. I'm surprised guards haven't come to check out the noise yet."

As if jinxing myself, two hulking minotaurs stepped into the chamber, weapons drawn.

"Gods above," I cursed.

"What?" Dormuris looked over his shoulder. "Oh, crap."

"You there," one of them shouted, pointing at us. "Halt!"

CHAPTER FOUR

Songful Words

"You carry the egg, I'll take the guards."

I leapt out of the nest, brandishing my sword. The minotaur who'd spoke came at me, his axe raised. I rolled to the left, away from his death stoke, and came up swinging. My face contorted in confusion as singing filled the chamber, throwing off my strike.

"Is that you?" I shouted at Dormuris.

"No!" he bellowed back.

"Pemeria?" I said aloud. I wasn't necessarily asking her, I was really just voicing my thoughts.

"No," her muffled voice replied. "Though it is lovely."

I didn't have time to think about it. The minotaur had recovered and was coming at me again. The other one stood by the door, blocking the exit. I dodged another viscous swing, then launched myself forward, stabbing the blade into the minotaur's armor. The mix of thick leather and chainmail kept me from drawing blood. I pulled the blade back quickly and heard the singing again.

> *"Weeeeeeell, a long time ago,*
> *in a valley of green,*

two adventurers were caught,
or so it did seem!"

What the f—

"It's the sword!" I shouted to the elf. "The sword is singing!"

How that was possible, I had no idea. It didn't even make sense, really. It was an inanimate object, but somehow it was singing about Dormuris and I. As I blocked the minotaurs strikes and thrusted forward with my own, the blade continued to sing.

"Seeking an egg of golden gleam,
they needed it badly,
more than they could dream!"

This was irritating. Every time I swung the blade, it belted out in song, describing our journey or what we were looking for. The minotaurs seemed amused at first, but as the sword sang about how we were going to steal an egg, their anger became evident.

"Crush the thieves!" the blind minotaur screeched.

From my peripheral, I could see the second minotaur guard lurching toward me. Now I was in real trouble. Two against one were difficult odds in general, but against two massive, horned beasts? I was pretty sure I was about to meet my end.

"Gods above," I whispered, "help me!"

Thunder rocked the entire chamber. The ground shook beneath my feet and I stumbled to my knees.

The two minotaur guards were more stable on their legs, but they seemed as confused as I was. Suddenly, frogs started raining from the ceiling. They were everywhere. I looked at Dormuris. He had set the egg down and was chanting and waving his arms.

"What is it with you and frogs?" I shouted. I scrambled backwards, away from the minotaurs, and watched as frogs covered the chamber floor. The creatures stepped on the frogs, crushing them and making the ground slick with blood. They toppled to the floor, falling on their axes. I grimaced. If that didn't kill them … I couldn't imagine the damage it caused.

"Come on! Let's get out of here!"

I reached down and patted the pouch that Pemeria was in. My heart dropped into my stomach. The pouch was empty! I looked down and saw several frogs. I panicked until I saw her. Snatching her up off the floor, I put her back in my pouch and ran for the doorway. Dormuris moved as quickly as he could, but the egg was huge and was going to slow us down. The blind minotaur staggered around, trying to join the fray. I peered into the tunnel.

There were no guards, but considering our luck, I wouldn't be surprised if they were on their way. Dormuris reached the door, huffing and puffing. It was obvious he was struggling, but if I carried the egg, there wouldn't be anyone to fend off the guards. I didn't trust his magic enough to keep us safe. He was as likely to kill us all as he was to rescue us.

I sheathed my blade and reached into Dormuris's pack to dig out the map. I found it and pulled it out, then unfolded it and traced the tunnel lines with my finger, trying to determine which way we should go.

"Bad news," I said. "We have to backtrack and take the same way out we got in here."

"Hopefully we won't encounter any guards on the way," Dormuris said.

"Hope in one hand and crap in the other and tell me which one fills up first," I replied.

"Why would I crap in my hand?" the elf asked, offended.

"It's a saying people use."

"You humans are disgusting."

"Yeah, well …" I didn't have an argument against that. It was true. Humans are disgusting. "Just, whatever. Let's go. If you start to lag behind, whistle so I can slow down."

Dormuris nodded. I led the way out of the chamber, carrying the map in my left hand in the event I needed to draw my sword. Since I knew there weren't many traps the way we had come, I let my urgency lead the way. Every so often, Dormuris would whistle and I would stop and wait for him to catch up.

We hadn't gone far and the elf's tunic was drenched in sweat. I could see his arms shaking with the exertion. I was about to offer to carry it when a minotaur stepped into the tunnel from a dimly illuminated corridor on the right. I stopped abruptly.

The massive creature ignored us and hurried past, heading the way we'd come. While I knew it was unlikely, I held the same hope Dormuris did about not running into any guards. As we neared the more populated areas, it was obvious that word had already spread like wildfire. The sound of hooved feet clattering on the stone floors, roars and shouts of anger filled the tunnel, echoing at every turn.

The gods must have been watching over us, for we had almost made it to the last tunnel before we saw another minotaur. It was the same one as before, the one who'd questioned us about patrolling the entrance. I slowed down and tried to walk in front of Dormuris to help hide the egg.

"You two again?" the beast questioned.

"Orders are orders," I grunted deeply. "Dadak said there's an intruder. He wants us at the entrance in case they get past everyone else."

The minotaur snorted. "No intruder would get past me, and there's only one way in."

I knew from reading the map that appeared to be true, but I knew too that it would be foolish of any leader not to have a secret escape route. It wasn't on the map, of course, but I was certain there was another way out.

"Dadak thinks they entered through the hidden

entrance."

The minotaur tilted his head. I smiled inwardly, knowing I'd piqued his interest.

"What hidden entrance?"

"Well, it's an exit, really. For the Triad to escape if anything ever goes south. Can't be too careful, you know? Anyway, duty calls."

I kept myself in front of Dormuris as we walked past the guard, doing my best to shield his body with mine. Once we turned the corner, we hurried as fast as Dormuris could walk. The air grew cooler as we neared the opening that led to the outside.

"Wait!"

I looked over my shoulder to see the minotaur closing in on us. Pushing Dormuris ahead, I fell behind and waited for the minotaur to catch up. He snorted, and I cringed as small bits of snot misted into the air.

"Do you know where this hidden door is?" he asked.

I shook my head. "No, I don't. I only heard Dadak mention it."

A slight tingle brushed my cheek. The minotaur's face scrunched in confusion, then surprise, then anger. I knew immediately that Dormuris's spell had faded. I shoved the map into my belt and drew my blade.

"Imposter!" the minotaur cried, drawing his enormous axe from its harness.

I retreated out of his reach and held my sword up defensively. The minotaur snorted and shook his head, then stamped his hoof forward and slid it back. Fear welled within me as the massive creature charged forward.

"Run!" I screamed to Dormuris, then I turned and sprinted as fast as I could. I passed the elf and latched my arm around him, pulling him along. The thunderous stomping was growing louder and closer.

Roughly a hundred feet ahead, I could see the cave opening. We were so close! I risked a glance back and saw the minotaur only a few paces away. The cave's opening drew closer, but we weren't going to make it. I shoved Dormuris aside, against the wall, and dropped to the ground. The rushing minotaur's muscular legs slammed into me and he tripped, crashing to the ground and skidding out onto the ledge.

I scrambled to my feet and pulled Pemeria out of the pouch. Surprisingly, she looked fine.

"Sorry!" I said, then tossed her towards Dormuris's feet.

My ribs burned something fierce, a few were probably broken. Forcing myself to move, I reached the ledge just as the minotaur was getting to his feet. I threw myself against him, sending jolts of sharp pain through my side, eliciting a scream born of pain and rage. I wasn't heavy enough to knock the beast over and he tossed me to the ground like I was a mere child.

The sword slipped from my grasp and went clattering off the ledge, my last bit of hope going with it. I tried to crawl backwards, staring up at the minotaur as he stalked forward, death gleaming in his dark eyes. This was it. This was how I was going to die. *If only I had my sword.*

And then suddenly, impossibly, the sword was there in my hand. I sat up and thrust it forward, striking the beast in the abdomen. He roared in agony and staggered back, clutching his wound. The minotaur staggered too far and slipped off the precipice, disappearing from sight. I dropped the blade and crawled forward to peer over the edge.

Far below, the minotaur slammed into the mountain, tumbling and smashing among the jagged rocks. I backed up and got to my feet, then headed into the cave. Dormuris was slumped against the wall, a cut above his eye dripping blood down his face. Other than that, he seemed all right.

"You dead?" I asked.

The elf laughed softly. "I'm fine. You?"

"I've suffered worse, believe it or not." I knelt and picked up Pemeria. "What about you?"

The frog croaked and looked at me, then hopped out of my hand. Dread filled me as I realized the frog I had grabbed wasn't Pemeria.

"Oh gods," I groaned.

"Don't tell me …" Dormuris trailed off, then closed his eyes. "We have to go back in," he said.

"You're damn right we do," I replied. "We can't leave her. She acted like me leaving her in the woods was the worst thing I could ever do. I can't imagine her anger if we left her with a bunch of oversized bulls."

"Stay here," I said. "I'll find her."

"You aren't in any shape to go in there alone," the elf argued. "I'm coming with you."

"We can't lug that egg back in there."

"You don't have to," Pemeria's voice echoed in the tunnel. She came hopping into the light. I knelt and picked her up, the heaviness in my chest disappearing like a brief storm.

"Thank the gods you're all right!"

"I tried calling to you in the room with the goose, but I guess you didn't hear me."

"I'm sorry," I said. "I didn't. It was chaos, though. Please forgive me for leaving you in there."

"I'll think about it," she answered.

I helped Dormuris to his feet and he rubbed the blood off his face with the sleeve of his robe. "Let's get going before anything else happens," I said.

I turned towards the ledge and stepped on the other frog. As soon as I felt it, I tried to lift my foot. It was hard to explain, but somehow my upper body and my legs didn't get the same message, and I went sprawling face first to the ground. And Pemeria? She tumbled from my hands and fell off the ledge.

CHAPTER FIVE

A Leap of Faith

"No!" I screamed.

I scrambled to my feet and looked, though I was afraid of what I would see. Pemeria was flying down through the air, quickly falling to her death. Dormuris was there beside me, holding the egg, a look of fear etched onto his face. Without thinking about the consequences, I pulled the wooden pendant from my boot, grabbed the elf's hand, and jumped off the ledge.

The womanliest scream came roaring out of Dormuris as we fell. I probably would have laughed if I didn't think this was complete suicide. The air whipped around me, deafening. I opened my mouth to cry out to Pemeria, but the wind forced my words back into my throat and my cheeks began to hurt as they flapped roughly. I tried to close my mouth, but it was almost impossible.

It felt like the rocky ground was coming up to meet us, speeding up faster and faster. I reached out and grabbed hold of Pemeria as we overtook her, then I broke the wooden pendant. At first, nothing happened. I remembered what Master Zalore said, about thinking of where you wanted to be. The ground was only fifty feet away, if that. I closed my eyes, not wanting to see my end, and pictured the Academy.

My stomach lurched, and I snapped my eyes back open. We were traveling through a portal, similar to the one that brought us to the Triad's mountain. The world shifted in and out of focus around us, and this time I thought I was going to be sick.

Everything slowed down, as if time itself were crawling, and then there was a *ploop* sound. A feeling of dizziness swept over me and I turned my head, expecting to vomit. I didn't, and the feeling passed. The world stopped spinning and I saw we were lying in the grass of a front courtyard. I sat up too quickly, immediately regretted it, and laid back down. I covered my eyes with my hand and recognized the architecture of the Academy.

We made it.

I laid still for a long moment, then eased myself up onto my feet. Pemeria was on the ground, looking up at me. She still looked angry, but that seemed to the be the case permanently since she'd been turned into a frog. I scooped her up and placed her back into my pouch, then looked for Dormuris. He stood a few feet away, clutching the oversized egg to his chest.

No guards came to investigate, so we made our way inside the building and up to Master Zalore's office. The door was open and he was sitting behind his desk, reading over the papers scattered upon its surface. He looked up as we entered and rose to his feet, an enormous smile spreading over his breaded face.

"You're back!" he said triumphantly.

"We are," I replied, trying to hide the fact that I was in pain.

"Where do you want this thing?" Dormuris huffed, struggling to keep from dropping the egg.

"I'll take it from here," Master Zalore answered. He whispered a few words and then motioned with his finger. The egg broke free of Dormuris's arms and hovered lazily past the old wizard's desk, onto a stone pedestal.

"That spell could have come in handy," I said, shooting a glance at Dormuris. The elf shrugged. Sharp pain lanced up my side. I clenched my jaw, trying to ignore it.

"That may have looked easy, but I can assure you it wasn't. Magic is not something just anyone can do. And for those with the gift, it is not easy to control. Dormuris here is not to be blamed for his lack of control. We are merely tools in the hands of magic, though others tend to believe the reverse."

I suddenly felt very light and my vision began to swim. "I don't—" the words abruptly ended and the last thing I saw before the darkness consumed me was the wooden floorboards of Master Zalore's office coming up to meet my face.

«—»

When I awoke, the first thing I noticed was that

everything was bright white. I soon realized I was lying on my back, staring up at the ceiling. I sat up and hissed as my side erupted in pain. I held my side tenderly and looked around.

An older woman dressed in gray robes was carrying a bowl, heading towards me. She smiled as she got close and set the bowl down on top of a table beside the bed I was on.

"I'm sure you're still in pain, but you'll heal up nicely. I did everything I could, but my magic is not what it once was. I managed to mend the broken ribs, but the muscles were bruised pretty bad. That's the pain you'll be feeling for a few days, but as long as you take it easy, you'll be back to normal in no time."

"Thanks," I said. Judging by the look of the room, I guessed I was in some sort of wizard infirmary.

The woman dipped a cloth into the bowl and wrung it out, then dabbed it against my temple. A stinging made me blink and wince, though it was nowhere near the pain of my side.

"They said you fell right on the floor," she said softly. "You had a nasty lump on your head, but the swelling is gone now. There's a small cut, but it doesn't look like its infected. I just want to be sure, though."

She hummed softly as she worked and I remembered the sword, how it crooned harmonically when I swung it. Dormuris had said the sword was enchanted with powerful magic. If singing was what he meant, he was crazier than I thought. Then again, when I dropped it fighting the minotaur, it had fallen off the ledge. Yet somehow, it magically came to me when I wished I had it. Was that one of the spells that it was charmed with?

I considered calling for it now, just to test my theory, but thought better of it. I'd hate for the old lady to get frightened or accidentally stabbed. Seeing as how she was a wizard, she probably wouldn't be frightened. She'd probably seen more scary things than I could imagine.

She finished her work and offered her arm to me. I accepted it, more to humor her than anything else. I didn't need her help to get off a bed. As soon as I was on my feet, I swooned with dizziness. On second thought, maybe I did need her help. The room spun for a moment, then everything calmed and I was able to walk without her assistance.

I was almost to the exit when Dormuris entered the room. His eyes widened and he seemed genuinely happy.

"I was wondering when you'd finally wake up. You had Pemeria worried."

"How long was I out?" I asked, confused.

"Two days," the elf answered. "Though it felt longer."

Two days? Holy gods!

"It didn't feel that long," I said.

"Do you need me to help you walk?"

"No," I answered. "My side hurts, but other than that I feel fine. Two days? Gods, what did I miss?"

"Not much," Dormuris said. "You passed out and went down hard. I thought for sure you cracked your skull open. Master Zalore called for the healers and they took you here. I've been watching over Pemeria while you were out. Master Zalore was happy we were able to get the egg. He says the quicker we can get the unicorn, the quicker he can change Pemeria back into her normal form."

"That's where we're going next," I said. "If we can steal an egg from the Triad and escape with our lives, catching a unicorn should be a walk in the woods."

"Have you ever seen a unicorn?" Dormuris asked.

"No, why?"

"They're large creatures. Bigger than horses, and an attitude problem you wouldn't believe. They used to be more common, but they were hunted for their horns and now most people think there's only a handful left."

"So, what you're saying is … this isn't going to be easy?"

Dormuris shook his head. "I'm afraid not."

"That's great," I sighed. Could one thing go right? Just one?

I followed Dormuris to the room he'd been given to stay in. My clothes were clean and neatly folded on a desk. I stripped out of the white robe I was wearing and put my own clothes on, then strapped my singing sword around my waist. Dormuris collected Pemeria, then we headed to Master Zalore's office. Again, we found him pouring over papers. When we entered this time, he didn't look up.

"You're alive," he said with a smile, but still didn't look up.

"It'll take more than a kick from a minotaur to take me down."

"That's good," he replied. "Because I have bad news."

"Bad news?" I repeated. "What's the problem?"

"Are you familiar with goblins?" Master Zalore asked, looking up.

"Extremely. I spent an entire summer hunting down a tribe of them a few years back. They're quick and spindly, but easy enough to kill."

"There's reports that a few have been spotted near Silverwood, which is where you'll need to go to find the unicorn. There should be three of them, a male and two females. I want one of the females. They are more docile than males, and more magical, too."

"Do you have to have an entire unicorn? Could you just use some of its hair or something?"

"No," Master Zalore shook his head. "I need the entire animal."

"How do we get it here?" I asked.

"The same way you got back from the Triad. I'll give you another pendant. Speaking of, you didn't use the last one when you were on the mountain, did you?"

I flashbacked to the moment I jumped off the ledge. Technically, we weren't *on* the mountain. "No," I lied.

"Good. If the minotaurs think the Academy had anything to do with the theft of one of their eggs, there's going to be hell to pay."

"I would think wizards could handle minotaurs without much fuss," I said. "Magic and all."

"We could, certainly, but you are missing out on the politics. Nevermind that," the old wizard waved his hand, as if pushing the subject away. "Silverwood is west of here, about three days on foot. Unfortunately, I won't be able to transport you as close to the woods as I would like. Unicorns are powerful and most magic doesn't work on or around them, so I'll have to drop you somewhere near Livaara."

I groaned inwardly. I'd been avoiding Livaara for months now. I suppose it wouldn't be too bad. It wasn't like we'd be staying in town. We were going to Silverwood, so it was doubtful I'd run into Theo and Breg. They were my old hunting partners and we'd been on bad terms for a while now.

"That should be fine," I said, not hearing the last bit Master Zalore said. "Is there any good news?"

"You've almost got your girlfriend back." The old wizard chuckled, apparently finding that funny. "Well, are you ready to go?" he asked.

"Now? I just woke up after being unconscious for two days."

"I know, but we don't have much time. If Pemeria stays in frog form too long, I won't be able to pull her out of it."

I was still in pain, but I'd struggled through worse. Like that time I accidentally stepped in my own bear trap when I was tracking a clan of meenlocks. Now *that* was a story.

"Dormuris, can you fill a pack with some food and water? Once you've got that, I guess I'm ready."

The elf left and then I remembered the man from Thurm. They had a vampire stealing their children. I looked at Master Zalore. "Can you get a letter to Lord Skrinn in Thurm?"

"Absolutely. A good friend of mine lives near there. I can have him deliver it personally. Do you want to write something, or should I?"

"Either," I answered. "I just need to let him know it's going to be a few more days before I can get there."

"Lord Skrinn summoned you?"

"In a way, yes. One of his townsfolk sought me out before we came here. They've got a monster that needs dealt with. A vampire."

Master Zalore nodded. "Fascinating! I've never studied monsters, but Master Verus is quite knowledgeable. When you get back with the unicorn, I can have him meet with you if you'd like to know anything about vampires? I've heard they are quite dangerous."

"So have I. And I would definitely like to pick his brain."

Dormuris returned carrying a pack that looked stuffed to the brim.

"Got enough supplies?" I asked, eyeing the bag.

"I think so."

I shrugged and looked at Master Zalore. "Let's get this over with," I said. "This whole travel by magic is not an ideal way to get around for me."

"Of course," the old wizard chuckled again. "Not everyone can handle flying through space and time. Here," he handed me a new pendant. This one was larger than the first one and had a symbol etched on the surface.

"Use it the same way you did the other one."

We walked over to where we had transported before. I watched as Master Zalore cast his magic, opening the swirling maelstrom entrance on the floor again. It seemed unnatural that a mortal should have access to such power. Then again, without magic it would be harder to kill certain monsters.

"Remember," Master Zalore said.

"Don't die," I finished his sentence with a

smirk.

"Of course, but I was going to say don't piss off the male unicorn. If he's feeling extra vengeful, he just might send you into another plane of existence."

I shook my head and jumped into the portal. Master Zalore smiled and waved and then everything disappeared.

CHAPTER SIX

Old Grudges Die Hard

As before, the magical portal gave me the sensation of falling, but it didn't last as long as before. I assumed this was due to the distance we traveled being shorter, but I really had no way of knowing that and I was certain neither did Dormuris.

I stood up and brushed my pants off. We'd landed on the outskirts of Livaara near the woods. The place looked the same, not that I thought it would have changed much in a couple of months. The familiarity of the place set me at ease, despite the fear I had of running into Theo and Breg.

Dormuris held up the pack he'd brought. It was empty and had a decent sized tear in the fabric.

"All of our supplies are gone," he said. "It must have ripped when we were in the portal."

"Well, we can't make the trip without food and water. Do you mind going into the town to get more? I'd rather not run the risk of bumping into my old hunter friends."

"I don't mind at all," the elf answered. "Is there any place in particular I should go?"

I shrugged. "Not really."

"I'll be back," Dormuris said and headed towards the road that led into Livaara. I forgot he was carrying Pemeria, so I was left to myself. I walked closer to the border of the town and stayed behind one of the taverns. After a few minutes of waiting, I felt the need to relieve myself, so I headed over to a thicket of bushes and pulled down the front of my pants.

As I was urinating, I heard a loud crash and raised voices. I finished my business, then turned around to see what was going on. I cursed my luck as I saw the two people I wanted to avoid, Theo and Breg, brawling with a group of other men. They were outnumbered, but Theo and Breg had the advantage.

They were brothers, with Theo being the oldest. Standing over six feet tall and each weighing almost as much as a minotaur, the brothers were an intimidating pair. That was part of the reason I had initially hired them. Typically the "muscle" of any group, their strength and brutality were the only thing that had saved the day many times. I turned and started to slink away when I heard Theo's booming voice.

"Well, look who it is, Breg."

I pretended not to hear him and kept walking. The loud thud of their footsteps grew closer. I could have ran, but my side was still hurting enough that I knew it would be a mistake. A heavy hand grabbed my shoulder and spun me around. Theo's big stupid grin was plastered on his face. He was missing one of his teeth, which always caught my attention when he smiled.

"Jack! What a surprise seeing you here. What brings you? Hopefully the money you owe us."

His tone was jovial, but I knew better than to assume he wasn't angry. I'd seen him kill a man with that smile on his face before. I glanced at Breg. Being the youngest, he tended to follow whatever Theo did. If Theo was angry, Breg was angry. His facial expression was hard to read.

"Oh, you know. I'm on a job and had to pass through."

"And you weren't going to stop and say hello to your good friends?"

"It's an urgent job," I said. "Life and death matter."

"Must pay a lot, then?"

"Actually, it's not a paid job."

"Gods above, Jack. Doing charity work now? I'm not as dumb as you think."

"I don't think you're dumb," I said. *I know you are,* I thought. "I'm telling you the truth."

"What's the job?" Theo's breath smelled like alcohol. He could be a real menace when he was drinking.

"Pemeria. You remember her, right? Well, she's been turned into a frog."

Theo stared at me for a moment, then burst into laughter. "Good one, Jack. You always know how to make me laugh."

"I'm serious," I said. "A wizard did it by accident. I've got to collect some things for a different wizard to turn her back."

Theo's laughter subsided. "Well, I'm sorry to tell you that she's going to be waiting a while. You aren't going anywhere until you pay up."

"I don't have any money on me," I argued.

"Breg," Theo said. "Let's show Jack here to our humble abode."

If trying to run was bad, trying to fight would be worse. Breg wrapped his muscled arm over my shoulders and pulled me with him. I'd never seen their home before. We usually were on the road hunting monsters, and when we weren't, we would split up and go our separate ways until a new job came in.

They led me to a small, squat and unadorned building near the center of town. We passed a shop and I spotted Dormuris, but his back was to me. If I couldn't find a way to ditch the brothers, he and Pemeria would probably panic when they couldn't find me.

"Theo, I don't have the money I owe you now, but if you let me go I can get some. I stole an egg from the Triad and I'm sure the wizard I gave it to would—"

"Hold up," Theo interrupted. Breg stopped walking, which made me stop walking since he still had his arm on me. "That heist was you?"

"It was," I said proudly. "Stole the egg and flew off like a bird. Literally."

"When I heard about that, I told Breg here that sounded like something you might do. Didn't I, Breg?"

Breg nodded. "Yep, you sure did."

Theo chuckled and shook his head. "You're in a lot of trouble for that, Jack. The Triad has put a bounty on your head. A hefty one, at that. And I think Breg and I are going to collect." His grin was devilish.

Damn.

I wouldn't be able to talk my way out of this one, not with the promise of money for turning me over to the Triad. I shuddered. If the Triad got their hands on me … I was a dead man for sure. Master Zalore had probably sealed my fate.

Time to figure out how to escape. Theo started walking again and Breg pulled me along. We went inside their house and Breg proceeded to tie me to a chair. That definitely put a hindrance in my plan of escape.

"Guys, I'm sure we can work something out."

"Unless it involves you paying us more than the Triad's bounty, I don't think we can," Theo said. He took a seat across from me and the chair creaked under his weight.

While Theo was the smarter of the two, he was still fairly dumb compared to most people. As long as I could convince him to do what I wanted, Breg would follow his brother's lead. So, the question was how to convince Theo to let me go? I met his eyes and hardened my gaze.

"How much is it going to take?" I asked. "If I match the amount the Triad is offering, would you let me go?"

Theo smirked and shook his head. "You already told us you don't have any money, Jack. If you weren't lying, where are you going to get a thousand gold coins?"

It took all of my effort not to let my mouth drop open in surprise. *A thousand gold coins?* That was a king's fortune! Where the hell would I get that kind of wealth? I tried to keep my composure.

"Well," I said, clearing my throat. "I have a new connection that can get me that much. Probably more." Dormuris would kill me if he knew I was pulling him into my personal debts. Then again, the elf owed me his life, right?

"Oh? And who would this connection be?"

"His name's Dormuris. He's an elven wizard."

Theo whistled and leaned back in his chair. "A wizard, huh? You've done something right if you've made a wizard a partner of yours. Does he know you don't pay up on your debts?"

"He owes me his life, so my personal business doesn't really concern him. He will do whatever I need until he fulfills his debt to me. So you see, Theo my friend, this could work out in your favor if you play your cards right."

I could see the wheels turning. Theo's tiny brain was trying to unwrap everything I said. If his brain really were powered by gears and such, smoke would have been coming out of his ears. There was a long moment of silence.

"How do I know you aren't lying to save your own skin?" he asked.

"What would I gain by lying to you? You know everything about me, so it wouldn't be hard for you to come find me if I hightailed it when you let me go."

"Prove it."

"Do what now?" I asked.

"Prove it. Prove that you really know this elf wizard."

"I can do that. We passed him on the way here."

Theo stood up. "What's he looked like? I'll go find him and bring him back here."

I sighed. I was hoping I could get away without actually involving Dormuris, but it looked like Theo was a bit brighter than I remembered. "Gray robes, pointy ears. He was in the general store getting some supplies for the job I'm doing."

"I'll be back," Theo said. He looked at his brother and nodded towards me. "Watch him. Don't let him do anything or go anywhere."

Breg nodded and took Theo's seat after he left. He stared at me and I stared around the room, then at the floor. It was hard to judge how much time passed, but it seemed like it was taking longer than it should have. I started to doze off but snapped my head up as the door opened and Theo and Dormuris entered the house.

"Found him," Theo said. "He was waiting outside town for you."

"Well, there's your proof," I said. "Now untie me."

"Not so fast," Theo said as Breg rose from his chair. "Just because there's an elf who knows you doesn't mean he's a wizard or that he can get the money you need."

Dormuris looked at me, curiosity on his face. I winked at him. "D, tell these gentlemen that you are a wizard and that you can get more than enough money to match the Triad's bounty."

The elf looked from me to Theo, then to Breg, and back to me. I could see the trepidation in his eyes, but he did well to hide it from the brothers.

"Yes, to both of those. Now, please untie him so we can be on our way."

"Show us your magic, elf. We aren't stupid. Jack has tricked us more times than I care to admit."

"I think you're exaggerating," I said, offended.

"Show us," Theo repeated, ignoring me.

Dormuris looked at me and I nodded my head. We both knew that his magic was probably going to make matters worse, but we didn't have any other options. Dormuris smiled and raised his arms. His sleeves fell backwards, revealing his tanned skin. He whispered a few words and pointed to the ropes that bound me. I expected something awful to happen to me, but instead I heard something in the fireplace. Theo's head turned so he could look. Amidst the black coals and ash, orange flames began to crackle. The fire started small, but quickly grew larger, filling the entire space.

"That's magic, all right," Theo said. "I believe it, Jack."

I was watching the look on Dormuris's face. He appeared to be straining, his face contorting into weird looks.

"Breg, untie—"

A thunderous *boom* resounded, and the entire house shook. A concussive blast knocked my chair over and I crashed to the ground on my injured side.

"Argh!" I growled. Pain lanced up my side, making my arm numb. I watched Dormuris stop chanting and shake his head, as if coming back to reality from some distant place. Then he looked at the damage and his eyes widened.

"A hand, if you don't mind," I wiggled, trying to ease the pressure on my side, but it wasn't working.

Dormuris knelt behind me and I felt the tightness of the ropes loosen. My arms were freed first, then the rest of my body. I crawled away from the chair and the elf helped me to my feet. The sharpness of the pain in my side diminished to an annoying throb. Theo and Breg were laying on the floor, unconscious.

"What were you trying to do?" I asked.

"I was trying to turn the ropes into coins," Dormuris answered. "I figured that would prove I was a wizard *and* give them this money you were talking about." He scowled.

"Yeah, about that," I said, rubbing my hand on the back of my neck. "I didn't think you would get directly involved here, so I said some things that I thought might convince them to let me go. I …" my words trailed off as I didn't know what to say. "I'm sorry," I finished lamely.

"It's fine," Dormuris replied. "We should probably get out of here before they wake up, though."

"Agreed."

We quickly left the house and headed down the street, back towards the hustle and bustle of the town's market area. I took the lead and led the elf to the left, away from the woods.

"Where are we going?" Dormuris asked.

"If I know Theo and Breg well enough, and I'm certain I do, they won't be out long. And they know the lay of the land here better than anyone. If we try to head for Silverwood now, they'll find us before we get far. So, we're going to lay low for a bit."

Despite the fact I hadn't been home in a long

while, I remembered my way around town fairly well. At the edge of the western side of town was an old church that was always open. We went inside and sat down among the rows of pews.

It was quiet. There was a peace the building exuded, if that made any sense. I slouched on the bench and stared at the statues that lined the upraised dais where the priest usually spoke from. Painful memories began to claw their way free of my emotional walls. This place had been a refuge for me as a child, and not necessarily for religious reasons. I knew the gods existed, but I didn't devote myself to any of them.

"Are you all right?"

I realized Dormuris was looking at me. A few tears rolled down my face and I quickly wiped them away. *Damn it.* Of course the elf would see me when I was weak. I nodded and turned to him.

"I'm fine. There's a lot of memories in this town, which is why I try to avoid it. I grew up here. My parents ... they were murdered here. A tribe of goblins raided when I was only a boy. I didn't see them get killed, thank the gods, but my uncle told me what happened. The city guard didn't exist then, so there were no defenses against anything like that.

"My uncle took me in and cared for me. I decided that day, when they died, that I would devote my life to hunting monsters and ending the torment they inflict on the innocent. The king sent soldiers here to train the men to fight. I spent most of my days learning from them. Wielding a sword, riding a horse, the things that soldiers learn. And the day I turned sixteen, I decided it was time for revenge."

I pulled an old, tattered armband loose that was wrapped around my belt and held it up. It was dirty and yellowed with age, but the symbol drawn in blood was still visible.

"Clan Whiteclaw," I said. "This was the clan responsible for the raid, the clan that killed my parents. On the day I planned to leave to find that goblin tribe, my uncle passed away. I took that as a sign that I was doing the right thing. I left everything I knew behind and started a new life."

"Did you find the goblins?" Dormuris asked quietly.

I nodded. "Yes. It took a few months, but eventually I tracked them down. I slaughtered every last one. I keep this as a reminder. Every time I have a moment of weakness, when I think that it would be easier to just lay down my sword, I look at this and remember my parents. And I remember why I fight, why I hunt monsters."

Dormuris remained silent, perhaps deep in thought. I pondered the next step in our journey. Silverwood was about an hour away. I didn't want to wait around Livaara too long. Traveling in the dark was rarely a good idea in general, and I didn't want to go into Silverwood blind. We stayed there in the church for a short while, enjoying the rest and the peace. Finally, I stood up and stretched.

"Let's go catch a unicorn," I said.

CHAPTER SEVEN

Goblins, Goblins, Everywhere

As we neared the border of Silverwood, I began to get the feeling that something wasn't right. I couldn't put my finger on it and I didn't see anything out of the ordinary, but the feeling was there. I've hunted monsters long enough to know that I should trust my instincts.

I led Dormuris off the path and into the thick undergrowth. It was slower going, but I wanted to be sure there was nothing to be concerned with. We came down a large hill when I smelled it. A sickly, sweet odor, like honey spilled over rotten eggs. The air grew warmer and ahead I spotted a small goblin camp.

We halted fifty feet from the camp and watched. There were five of the spindly creatures. One was playing chef, turning what appeared to be a spitted deer over a fire. One was standing watch at the other end of the camp. Two sat beside an animal skin tent playing a game with teeth and bone fragments. The fifth one was sharpening a wicked looking sword.

"*Gods above,*" Dormuris gagged. "What's that stench?"

"Goblin," I whispered in reply. "And keep your

voice down. They have excellent hearing."

I studied the layout of their camp. It was new and, judging by the material their tent was made of, temporary. I wondered what they were doing out here. Goblins typically live in communes of dense populations, usually in underground caves. They're small and mostly considered a nuisance, but in large numbers they can easily overtake a small town.

These ones all seemed to be from different tribes. I could tell because of their varying skin color. Goblins of the same tribe have the same color, which can range from yellow to orange. A few are known to have green, but I've never seen a green one before. The one sharpening his sword looked like the common type I had killed before.

Flat face, broad nose, pointed ears, and small, sharp fangs. He was dressed in dark leathers, stained and soiled by his poor hygiene. He was average size for a goblin, so I guessed he stood just under four feet tall. He seemed likely to put up the most fight, so I decided to go for him first.

The goblin stood up and tossed his whetstone to the ground, then swung his sword a few times. The air whistled softly, and he seemed satisfied. Sheathing the blade, he walked over and sniffed the deer that was cooking.

"We're going to have to move quickly," I said. "Goblins are swift and stealthy. If they get the chance, they'll make like the wind and disappear into hiding."

"What do you want me to do?" Dormuris asked.

"I could cast a fireball—"

"Absolutely not," I whispered harshly. "Why would fire be your first idea in a forest?"

The elf shrugged.

"No, do not cast any spells. I'll kill them all. If any get away, just keep track of which direction they go. There must be a larger camp somewhere. This isn't even enough goblins to be considered a hunting party."

"Got it."

I took a deep breath and slowly slipped closer to their camp. Considering that the muscles in my side still hurt, I wasn't sure how well this was going to end up. I drew my blade and made sure not to swing it about too fast. The last thing I needed was my sword singing about how I was going to kill them and blowing my element of surprise.

My main concern was the one standing watch. He was the furthest away and would be the most likely to escape and sound the alarm. I ordered my priorities: sword goblin, watch guard, chef, game players.

Inhale, exhale. Inhale, exhale. Go!

I sprinted from the cover of the brush and headed straight for sword goblin. My sword arced up high, then came down in a diagonal swing. The blade began belting out vocal music as it rived through the lanky creature's body, tearing through its meager armor and into flesh and bone. He was dead before he knew I was on him.

Watch guard was next. I sprinted through the camp to the other side. He must have heard my pounding footsteps, for he turned as I struck him a death blow. I turned back toward the remaining three. Their surprise and shock were gone and now they were whooping with excitement. Chef grabbed a spear and the other two were on their feet, one wielding a mace and the other two daggers.

Chef hurled the spear at me, but it was crudely made and wobbled wildly in the air. It landed on the ground in front of me. I picked it up, cut it in half with my sword, and hurled it back. It was less wobbly, but the goblin leapt out of the way and the projectile stuck harmlessly into the soft ground.

The one wielding the mace ran at me, no apparent fear at all. He swung the weapon in a rage, forcing me to back away. I held my sword up defensively, and tried to circle around him, but he was quick. He rushed me, holding the mace above his head. I rolled to the side, much to my discomfort, and came up with a flourish, swinging the blade out wide and cutting the goblin's abdomen open.

> *"Goblins, goblins, everywhere!*
> *There's just too many,*
> *Let's get out of here!"*

Intestines, blood and organs spilled out onto the ground. The goblin fell into his own mess, his lifeless grip still clutching the mace. Was my sword scared of a few goblins? I shook my head and leapt over the body and headed for the dagger wielding one. He chattered at the other one in their guttural language, the Chef sprinted for the woods.

I lunged forward and thrust my sword at the goblin's chest. It struck him, but his rusty chainmail kept the damage minimal. He slashed at me with both daggers, each from a different direction. I jerked my sword up and to the right to block the first one, but he managed to slit my left arm with the other. It wasn't deep, but it stung like hell.

The goblin, seeing blood, went into a frenzy. His tiny arms flailed eagerly, trying to score another hit. I back peddled, slapping his daggers aside when they got too close for comfort. Maybe if I let the little thing wear itself out, I could get past his offensive fury. Then I remembered Chef was probably going for help.

"Blast it," I cursed, then threw my sword at the goblin. It squealed in surprise. The blade flipped end over end and slammed into the ugly creature's face, hilt first. I heard the crack of bone and the goblin froze, then staggered back a few steps. Blood began pouring freely from its nose.

It blinked several times, still reeling from the force of the blow. I tackled him and both of us crashed to the ground. My injured muscles cried out in agony, but my adrenaline was pumping and forced the pain out of my mind. I wrested one of the daggers from the goblin and rammed the blade into its throat. It gurgled a weak, wet cry and then lay still.

I staggered to my feet and grabbed my sword, then ran in the direction of Chef. I figured he ran for the main group, but I was surprised to find him cowering behind a large tree not far from the camp. I removed his head from his shoulders and returned to where Dormuris waited.

"That was intense," he said. "And violent. Very violent."

"If you give them an inch, they'll take your life," I replied. "Goblins are small and weak, but they are vicious. They're worse than trolls, in my opinion. Let's see if they have anything we can use."

I entered the tent to find a single chest. It was a foot long, half a foot deep, and half a foot tall. No beds, no supplies, nothing. I knew there had to be another group somewhere close. I knelt and opened the chest, then whistled in surprise.

"What'd you find?" Dormuris called from outside the shelter.

"Gold," I answered. "Lots of it."

I picked up a coin and frowned. It had the image of a minotaur on it. Why would goblins have minotaur gold? They were hated enemies. Something was definitely wrong here. I hefted the chest and carried it out of the tent.

"That is a lot of gold," Dormuris said.

"I want to see!" Pemeria's muffled voice added.

Dormuris pulled her out of his robes and held her up to the chest.

"That *is* a lot," she breathed.

"It's minotaur gold," I said. "Something bad is going on here."

"What do we do with it?" Dormuris asked.

"Keep it," I said, shrugging. "We can't take it with us right now, but we can bury it and come back for it."

"I'll dig the hole," Dormuris offered. He grabbed the spear I had thrown and quickly dug a hole in the ground at the base of a large tree. It didn't take him long, mainly because the ground was so soft. We put the chest in the hole, then buried it and covered it with leaves.

"I just hope we can find it when we come back," the elf said.

"We will."

I cut a strip of my shirt off and wrapped it around my arm as a makeshift bandage, then we headed north out of the goblin camp which took us up a steep hill. It was difficult, but we made it to the top. The air was humid under the trees and I was soaked with sweat. Dormuris sat on a rock to rest, but I stepped out of the trees and looked down into the valley below. I think my heart stopped beating momentarily at what I saw. It made sense now, what the sword had sung.

"Goblins, goblins, everywhere," I whispered.

There were at least a hundred, maybe more. Makeshift tents like the one back at the camp littered the valley, darkening the landscape like a plague. In the center of the goblin army was a red pulsing light. I wasn't quite sure, but there appeared to be three white horses around that light.

"D," I said without turning. "We've got a problem."

"When don't we have a problem?" the elf asked as he came to stand beside me. "Gods above," he gasped.

"I'm not sure how we can enter Silverwood with this in the way," I said.

"We don't need to enter Silverwood," Dormuris replied. "They have the unicorns. All three."

I squinted into the distance but was unable to make out any details. Elves have incredible vision, so Dormuris was able to see the details I couldn't.

"I thought those white things were horses," I said.

"No, they are unicorns. There's something odd, though. They are staring at some sort of red stone and aren't moving at all."

The only way to get to the unicorns was to go straight into the camp. I frowned and considered our options, which were few. As much as I dreaded it, we were going to need Theo and Breg. The chest of gold would be more than enough to convince them to help. I looked at Dormuris.

"We're going to need help."

He returned my gaze and nodded slowly. "I'll cast a fireball."

"What? No. What is with you and fire? And

frogs?"

Dormuris shrugged.

"I mean, we need Theo and Breg."

"We just got away from those lunatics! Now you want to go back and ask for their help? Besides, we need an entire army. Look how many there are!"

"We don't have an army," I replied. "And since this is so far from Livaara, the Lord won't send the city guard out here. We'll have to deal with this ourselves."

"I don't think they are going to help," Dormuris argued. "They'll probably take you straight to the minotaurs this time."

"Not if I give them the chest," I said.

"I wanted to spend that," Pemeria's voice came out of the elf's robes.

"Do you want to be human again?" I asked.

"Of course I do," she shot back.

"Then we have to give them the gold."

"Fine," she groaned.

«—»

I kicked the door to Theo and Breg's house open, which I immediately regretted.

The jolt sent a ripple of pain through my side. I cursed silently and stepped inside. The giant brothers were sitting at a table and snapped their heads up.

"Well, well, well," Theo grunted, standing to his feet. "Look who's ready to die."

I flung a bag of gold at him. He snatched it out of the air and looked inside. I tossed another bag to Breg. Theo looked at me and smiled.

"That should be more than enough to cover what I owe you, as well as the addition of the Triad's bounty."

"Aye," Theo said. "We'll call it square, won't we, Breg?"

"Squared," Breg replied.

"I've got more if you're interested in working with me again." I let the offer hang in the air. Money was the driving force for some people, and Theo was one of them. He walked over to Breg and they engaged in a whispered conversation, then Theo looked at me.

"What's it pay?" he asked.

"Same amount I just gave you." Dormuris and I had divided the coins into three piles, two for Theo and Breg, one for us to split. I put half of the piles into each of the brother's bags with the hopes that they would agree to helping with the guarantee of more money.

Theo's brows rose in disbelief. "We're in," he said. "What's the job?"

"It's a death's mission," I warned. "There's an army of goblins outside Silverwood that needs to be cleared."

"Goblins, eh? I can deal with goblins," Theo said. "Can't we, Breg?"

"Yeah," his brother answered. "I love killin' goblins."

"Good. Let's get to work."

With them paid off and on board for helping, I heaved a sigh of relief. Still, this was going to be harder than it seemed.

CHAPTER EIGHT

Death Comes Quickly

Dormuris and I made our way carefully down the hill towards the goblin army. The elf still had Pemeria in his robes, which I didn't like, but there was nowhere else she could safety be kept. I didn't trust leaving her at Theo's house. Any number of things could happen. At least here with me, I could be aware of her safety.

Theo and Breg had circled around to the other side of the camp. The plan was to attack them from both sides, though Dormuris would stay out of sight. He offered to use his magic, but I wasn't comfortable with that. As it stood, he was one for three with his spells. I didn't like those odds. And so, it was three men against an army of goblins.

I drew my blade and waited for the signal that Theo and Breg were in place. Being closer to the camp afforded me a better view of the unicorns and the camp layout. The horned creatures stood completely immobile, staring fixedly at the pulsing red stone between them.

"Magic," Dormuris whispered beside me.

"What?"

"Magic," he repeated, nodding toward the glowing stone. "That thing is powered by magic.

Powerful magic, too. I can feel it tingling my skin from here."

Now that he said something, I could faintly feel it, too. "Goblins have shamans, which is essentially the human equivalent of a wizard," I said. "They aren't very strong or smart, so I don't think they are behind whatever that is."

"I agree," the elf said. "Someone much stronger is behind that."

Dormuris's ominous words added to my feeling of something not being right. A gathering this large of goblins *was* out of the ordinary, but with the addition of minotaur gold and powerful magic, I had a suspicion something much larger was going on. It wasn't my responsibility to unravel whatever that might be, but it was hindering me getting Pemeria back into her human form again.

Theo should have given the signal by now. I began to wonder if something had gone wrong. Did goblin scouts spot them? Did they get captured? A raucous erupted on the far side of the camp, but the tents blocked my view.

"I'll assume that's the signal," I grunted.

I sprinted across the open valley towards the encampment, my blade angled back behind me in case I tripped. I didn't want to impale myself if that happened. I reached the edge of the camp without notice, mainly because whatever was going on at the other side had drawn the attention of the entire camp.

Zig-zagging between tents, I managed to work my way to the pen holding the unicorns. I could feel the pulsing of the magic stone more profoundly now. There was a buzzing sound in the air, too. The unicorns were much bigger than they looked from a distance. Easily taller than a normal horse, they towered over me like giants. Their horns were long, probably a full foot in length, with a twisting pattern that glimmered in the sun.

Their eyes were glazed with a red tint, leading me to suspect that whatever that stone was, it had somehow captured their minds. A screech caught my attention and I looked over to see a goblin pointing its spear towards me. He shouted over his shoulder, then charged me.

"Great," I muttered. I was hoping to get in and out with little difficulty. Of course, nothing ever went according to plan. Once the goblin was close enough, I swung my blade and chopped the tip of the spear off. The metal end *clinked* as it hit the ground. I closed the gap between us and drove the blade into the goblin's chest. It shrieked in agony and collapsed, falling off my blade. I wiped the blood on the creature's dirty armor and noticed a contingent of the goblins rushing my way.

Theo's familiar battle cry echoed over the noise and I knew that he and Breg were dealing death to the goblins on the other side of the camp. I stepped away from the fallen goblin and set my feet firmly in the ground, taking a defensive stance. I brought my blade up horizontally before me, ready for the onslaught.

The small beasts crowded around me, hacking and slashing wildly. I took a few cuts to my legs and arms, but they weren't bad. I thrusted this way and that, stabbing one goblin in its eye and another in the neck.

One of them dropped to the ground, crawling forward on its hands and knees. It latched onto my leg and bit me. I jerked my leg in surprise, resulting in the goblin getting a mouthful of flesh. Burning pain shot up my leg and I kicked the creature in the face, smashing its nose and lips. Blood gushed from its mouth, but it could have been mine.

I tried to keep my weight off that leg and swung my sword in a wide circle, slicing wooden spears and goblin arms. Shrieks of pain and anger filled the air as the creatures fell before my singing blade.

> *"The hero cut them until they were sour,*
> *But their minotaur friend was humming,*
> *Magic and mayhem, gold and power,*
> *Here he is, here he is, incoming!"*

The ground shook beneath my feet. I looked up and saw a behemoth charging through the camp. It was a minotaur clothed in chainmail and leathers, wielding a staff. He trampled over a few goblins unlucky enough to be in his way.

I shoved a goblin and dove to the ground, away from the monstrous beast. It tried to slow its momentum but smashed through the remaining goblins before slowing enough to turn around. I scrambled to my feet, the wound on my leg burning fiercely. The minotaur roared mightily. It was gargantuan in size, standing a full three feet taller than me. I thought the unicorns made me feel small, but this beast made me feel like a dwarf. I didn't have a chance.

He knew it. I knew it.

For the first time in my life, I ran. I dashed across the camp in the direction of Theo and Breg. We had a better chance of taking the creature down with a concentrated effort. The area around the brothers was littered with both goblin bodies and limbs. The brothers stood back to back, smashing and pulverizing the mass of goblins that surrounded them. I joined the fray, cutting a path with my blade.

"We've got a problem!" I shouted.

Theo wielded a giant longsword. He swung the thing like a club, left to right, and cut down six goblins. Those standing behind their fallen comrades backed up, second-guessing if they wanted to close in. Theo looked past me to the minotaur thundering toward us. For a split second, his face betrayed his stoic exterior. It was fleeting, but it was there: *fear*.

The minotaur lowered its shoulder and charged straight into the mass of bodies. He clipped me and I spun in a circle, then fell atop a pile of goblins. Most of them were dead, but a few were only injured and squirmed beneath me. I drove my fist into a throat and ran my sword through an abdomen as I got up.

Theo and Breg were trading blows with the

minotaur, their weapons on the ground. At first, it seemed that they were holding their own against the brute. It quickly became clear the beast had the advantage. He knocked Theo with a solid blow to the face, sending the big man staggering backwards. Theo crashed to the ground on his back.

Breg roared a battle cry and punched the minotaur in the chest, then in the side of its face. It didn't seem to affect the beast at all. I stormed ahead, swinging my blade at the minotaur's legs. At the last moment, the blade suddenly diverted and struck the ground. Some sort of invisible barrier kept me from striking the minotaur.

"Magic," I whispered, realizing this creature was the source of it. The air around him thrummed with power. I swung again and again, thinking to wear down the spell. The barrier continued to divert my blade each time, with no sign of weakening. The minotaur struck Breg with a mighty blow and the big man collapsed in a spray of blood from his broken nose. The beast turned to me.

This was it. The end of my life, here in this valley filled with goblins. I imagined my end being much different. I think we all do. I braced myself and brought my blade up, willing to face death boldly.

Theo's body came hurtling through the air and he crashed into the minotaur, forcing the creature to stumble and fall to its knees. The big man rolled away and I swung my sword, seeking to behead the minotaur. Again, my blade was deflected. The minotaur snorted and rose back to its feet.

"Gods above!" I cursed. "I can't kill the damn thing!"

"Look out!" Theo cried.

The minotaur had picked up its staff and swung the bottom end of it at me. I moved my head in time to keep from getting my face smashed, but I took the brunt of the blow to my right shoulder. The jarring force knocked it out of its socket and the sword dropped from my limp grasp. My fingers went numb and an excruciating pain flooded my entire arm. The pain was too much, and I crumpled to the ground.

My eyes blurred with tears, but I could see enough to watch Theo strike the minotaur in the face. I was dizzy even though I was lying on the ground, and odd thoughts started creeping into my mind.

I'm dying. My shoulder is killing me. It's turned against my body and is waging its own battle. I have to pee. I'm hungry.

In the haze of my thoughts and the pain in my shoulder, I became aware of Dormuris standing over me. My face scrunched in confusion, not sure when he'd arrived at the battlefield. And why was he here? Didn't I tell him to stay hidden, to keep Pemeria safe?

"D," I gasped. It must have been too low, because he didn't turn to face me.

"Unhand him, vile creature of darkness!" Dormuris's voice thundered across the valley. It's entirely possible I imagined everything that followed, considering the pain I was in. I think I went into shock.

The minotaur roared and pointed its staff at the elf. A wave of fire spewed from the end of the wooden pole, striking Dormuris full on. I tried to cry out at his death, but no words left my mouth. The flames faded, and I was surprised to see that the elf was still standing there. Not even his robes were singed.

Dormuris chanted the words to a spell and my anxiety flared. He was probably going to kill us all. On accident.

A flash of lightning roared down from the sky, momentarily blinding me. As the white light faded, I saw the blast had struck the minotaur and thrown him to the ground. The beast got back up and a sickly green light flared from the top of its staff, bathing the area with its bizarre hue. Dormuris raised his arm up and covered his eyes, and the minotaur charged toward him. I wished I had my sword and that I could stand and fight.

I felt the blade in my hand and the hazy memory of the same thing happening back at the mountain tugged at my mind. Was it possible the sword knew my thoughts? If I could somehow summon the blade, could I send it somewhere else? I willed it to fly from my hand and strike the minotaur.

The sword stayed in my hand.

As the minotaur rammed into Dormuris, the elf's robes were suddenly empty and wrapped around the beast, whipping about wildly. He was gone. I blinked a few times, thinking I was seeing things. No, the elf was gone. The image of a naked Dormuris wandering around without his robes assaulted my mind.

Gods above, I thought to myself. *That's horrid!*

And then Dormuris was there again, fully clothed. I felt just as confused as the minotaur looked. The elf raised his hand and chanted again. Three white globes of light materialized in front of his raised hand and sped forth, striking the minotaur in the chest. For the first time, the creature roared in pain.

I struggled to sit up and vomited. The dizziness faded enough that I managed to get on my feet. I gripped my sword in my left hand and staggered forward, the pain in my leg making me limp. Dormuris and the minotaur were flinging spells back and forth at one another. Knowing that was a battle I couldn't contend in, I headed for the pen holding the unicorns.

The gate was unlatched, but I didn't have the strength to push it open. The wooden beams that formed the fence were wide enough to slip through, so I did just that. I cried out in discomfort when I bumped my shoulder against the top rail, but otherwise made it through without too much difficulty. The stone was attached to a wooden pole that had been driven into the ground.

The light pulsed rhythmically, and the air hummed in tune with it. The unicorns were still ensorcelled by its power, but there had to be a way to break the trance. A roar echoed across the valley, followed by an explosion. I lifted my sword up awkwardly, not used to using my left arm. I placed the tip of the blade against the stone and pushed. The pole it stood on was stable and didn't budge.

I tried kicking the pole, but that just made my pain worse. As I stood there trying to figure out a way to free the unicorns, an idea came to me. I lifted my blade and placed it in the male unicorn's line of sight, blocking the stone from its view.

Nothing happened.

The red glaze in its eyes was still there. I held the blade in place as long as I could before tremors began to make my arm twitch from exertion. Just as I was about to give up, the haze in the unicorn's eyes faded and the beast took a step back.

"Yes!" I said aloud and lowered my blade.

The towering horned creature looked down at me, looking rather sleepy. It blinked several times and shook its head, then snorted. It met my gaze and I felt a tingle against my leg and my shoulder, much like the tingle I'd felt when Dormuris had cast his minotaur illusion on me. The pain subsided, and my body flooded with relief. The unicorn spoke to me, though not audibly. It was in my mind, an extrasensory experience.

Where is the minotaur? It asked.

I pointed to where Dormuris was battling with it. The unicorn turned around and leapt over the wall of the pen in a single bound, then raced off. I rolled my shoulder and was surprised to feel no pain. I looked at the two females and wondered how the male unicorn was going to feel when we hauled off one of them.

With my strength restored, I cut the pole in half and the top portion holding the stone clattered to the ground. I picked it up by the end and slammed the stone onto the ground, shattering it into a hundred pieces.

The red light died, and the unicorns came back to reality. I backed away from them and opened the gate, then headed towards the fight. Dormuris was nowhere to be seen. Theo and Breg were gone as well. The minotaur lay on the ground, gored to death by the unicorn. It trotted away, back towards the females.

I looked around the encampment. It was empty now. There were many bodies, but many more of the creatures were nowhere to be seen. They must have fled in fear. Goblins weren't known for their bravery. I walked back towards the pen, trying to figure out how we could take one of the females without the male turning on us. I had no ideas.

Dormuris was standing near the pen, though he kept his distance. I stood beside him and lowered my voice.

"How do we do this?" I asked.

"Carefully," he replied.

"I figured that."

The male unicorn turned toward Silverwood and sped off. The two females followed, though at a much slower pace. One of them stopped and turned back toward us. I pulled the pendant Master Zalore gave me and held it in my hand at my side. The unicorn came trotting over and nuzzled me. It went to do the same thing to Dormuris, but I snapped the pendant in half and everything around us distorted.

CHAPTER NINE

An Unexpected Ending

I was on my back, staring up at the sky.

That seemed to be the normal result every time we traveled by magic. I got up and saw Dormuris petting the unicorn, though she seemed to be distracted by something.

"What's happening?" I asked.

"She's disoriented," the elf answered.

"I thought Master Zalore said unicorns weren't affected by magic."

"*Most* magic," Master Zalore's voice answered. I turned to see the old wizard approaching us. "And that is true. It isn't the transport spell that's affecting her, it's my spell."

He smiled and patted the unicorn's muscled neck. "She's more beautiful than I could have imagined. Good work. Let's take her to the stables for now."

Dormuris guided the animal there and I walked beside the old man. "Now that we have the egg and unicorn, you can turn Pemeria back into a human?" I asked.

"Absolutely," he answered.

"When? Now?"

"As soon as we get to my office," he replied.

Dormuris handed the unicorn off to the stable boys and then we went inside and followed Master Zalore to his office. Dormuris pulled Pemeria out of his robes and handed her to me. She looked up at me, the anger less than before, but I could tell she wasn't over the whole ordeal.

"Where should I put her?" I asked.

"On the floor, unless you think you can hold her entire body in your hand when she changes."

That imagery made me smile and I set her gently on the floor, then stepped back next to Dormuris.

Master Zalore pulled a book off his desk, flipped through a couple of pages, then stopped and ran his finger over the text. Nodding to himself, he looked at Pemeria and spoke something unintelligible.

There was a flash of light and some smoke, and then Pemeria was standing there, human again. I rushed forward and embraced her, crushing her tightly against me. She returned the hug, but there was less enthusiasm on her end. I pulled back and looked at her.

"What's wrong?" I asked.

"What's wrong?" she repeated. "What's wrong, you ask? Well, Jack, I've been a frog for the last few days. And on top of *that,* I've been carried around like some sort of burden. I'm sorry, but I can't do this anymore. I thought I wanted to marry you, but this little adventure has shown me that you aren't ready for that."

Pemeria wiped a tear from her eye and shook her head. "I'm sorry, Jack, but I'm leaving."

And just like that, she left the room and disappeared into the hall. I stood there, more than slightly confused, but also not really surprised. Pemeria over reacted all the time. I just needed to give her some space and, in a few days, she'd be right as the rain. I looked at Master Zalore, who looked like he felt a bit awkward seeing Pemeria's outburst.

"Don't worry about her," I said. "She'll calm down." I hope.

"How did you do the spell without the egg or the unicorn?" I asked.

"Oh, right! I didn't need them as components to the spell," he answered.

"Do what now?"

"Yeah, I just wanted to be rich and have a unicorn. I mean, who wouldn't want to ride around on a unicorn, right?"

I looked at Dormuris, who shrugged.

"We risked our lives for those things," I said, still expecting the old wizard to say he was joking.

"I know, and I really appreciate that. I'll be the talk of the Academy for years to come, all thanks to you two! Oh! This came for you." He handed me a folded parchment.

I took it. Doubly confused now, I left Master Zalore's office. Dormuris followed behind me and we left the Academy behind, stopping at a tavern. I needed a drink.

"Did we really just do all of that … for nothing?" I asked.

"Sounds like it," the elf answered.

We sat at a table and drank in silence. I still couldn't believe that old bastard tricked us, but what could we do? Did we even need to do anything? I shook my head and unfolded the parchment. It was a letter from Lord Skrinn, short and simple.

Jack,

Please make haste. The vampire has taken more of our children.

Lord Skrinn

"What is it?" Dormuris asked, watching me.

I downed the rest of my drink. If the last few days had taught me anything, it was that things never went according to plan. That didn't mean I didn't need a plan, of course. I did. Especially considering the type of creature we would have to face. Trolls, goblins, minotaurs. Those were child's play in comparison. I stood up and cracked my neck.

"Let's go hunt down a vampire," I answered.

THE END

ABOUT THE AUTHOR

Richard Fierce is a fantasy author best known for his novella *The Last Page*. He's been writing since childhood, but became seriously vested in it in 2007. Since then, he's written 7 novels and a few short stories.

In 2000, Richard won Poet of the Year for his poem *The Darkness*. He's also one of the creative brains behind the Allatoona Book Festival, a literary event in Acworth, Georgia.

A recovering retail worker, he now works in the tech industry when he's not busy writing.

He has three step-daughters, three huskies, three cats, two birds and a hamster.

His love affair with fantasy was born in high school when a friend's mother gave him a copy of *Dragons of Spring Dawning* by Margaret Weis and Tracy Hickman.

www.ingramcontent.com/pod-product-compliance
Lightning Source LLC
Chambersburg PA
CBHW032018180726
48283CB00008B/2737